FIASCO AT THE JAM FACTORY

Churchill and Pemberley Mystery Book 7

EMILY ORGAN

emilyorgan.com

ISBN 978-1-8384931-8-9

Fiasco at the Jam Factory

Emily Organ

Books in the Churchill & Pemberley Series:
Tragedy at Piddleton Hotel
Murder in Cold Mud
Puzzle in Poppleford Wood
Trouble in the Churchyard
Wheels of Peril
The Poisoned Peer
Fiasco at the Jam Factory

Christmas Calamity at the Vicarage - a novella

Chapter 1

"MUST you read a book while we're enjoying elevenses, Pembers?" private detective Annabel Churchill said to her trusty assistant as she buttered a scone. "It puts a bit of a dampener on our conversation."

The two ladies were seated at a little table in Compton Poppleford's popular tea rooms.

"Oh, I am sorry, Mrs Churchill." Doris Pemberley put her book down. "I can't help it, you see. It's so terribly gripping."

"What's it about?"

"A heist at an art gallery. Lightfinger Jones and his team are currently creeping along a corridor in the dark, and they've just spotted a security guard approaching with a torch. I'm so worried he's going to discover them!"

"I wouldn't worry too much, Pembers. It's not real, you know."

"But it *feels* real. Don't you find that with some books? Sometimes they seem so real you feel like you're part of the story."

"Perhaps I should give your book a try. What's it called?"

"*The Havana Heist.*"

"I like the sound of that." Churchill spread some jam on top of the butter.

"You should read it, Mrs Churchill. It'll make a nice change from those racy romances Mrs Thonnings lends you."

"There's nothing wrong with *Forbidden Obsession*, Pembers. It actually has a decent plot, contrary to some people's preconceptions. It's usually the sort of people who've never read such books in the first place who choose to comment. What's wrong with a little romance, anyway? We need a good deal more of it in this troubled world, I say."

"But not in Compton Poppleford."

"Why not?"

"Is there anyone you could envisage having a romance with around here, Mrs Churchill?"

"What a question! Absolutely not."

"There you go. There can be no romance in Compton Poppleford."

"At least not for us, Pembers. Mrs Thonnings certainly manages to keep the fire burning. I really don't know how she does it." Churchill bit into her scone.

"She wears fancy blouses," said Pemberley, "and pretty tea dresses."

"I'd wear a pretty tea dress myself if I could find one that didn't make me look like a saggy summer pudding. Oh dear. Have you tried the jam yet? It tastes rather bland."

"It doesn't have enough sugar in it. Or enough fruit, for that matter."

"The two main ingredients, one might say. What a disappointment."

"I imagine it's from Lidcup's," said Pemberley. "Perhaps they've produced a dodgy batch."

"There's no *perhaps* about it. It's quite clear they've produced a dodgy batch, Pembers. Never mind; at least the scones are good. Let's eat up. We have a busy day ahead of us."

"Do we?"

"Yes. We need to reorganise our files."

"That doesn't sound very interesting." Pemberley fed the remains of her scone to her scruffy little dog, Oswald, who was sitting beneath the table. "I wonder when we'll have our next gripping case to work on."

"It'll come along soon enough, Pembers. It always does. Just enjoy the peaceful lull in between."

It turned out the lull was short-lived. As the two ladies and their dog stepped out onto the high street, there was noticeable excitement in the air. A crowd of people appeared to be striding toward the far end of the high street, while numerous ladies carrying shopping baskets stood huddled in groups. Mrs Crackleby had abandoned her flower stall for an urgent conflab with the village haberdasher, Mrs Thonnings, and the greengrocer's wife, Mrs Harris.

"Something's afoot," commented Churchill. "Do you sense it, Pembers?"

"Yes, I do. I wonder what's happened."

They approached the nearest group of ladies.

"I thought it was the day of reckoning!" exclaimed Mrs Thonnings. Her artificially red-tinged hair had tumbled into her face, as if the drama were too much for it.

"I thought the sky had fallen in!" added Mrs Harris, her large front teeth protruding more than ever.

"I want to know how it fell," said Mrs Crackleby.

"It must have just got old and rusty," replied Mrs Thonnings. "It's a very bad business indeed. The vicar should have been checking it! People never check things these days, do they? Oh, hello Mrs Churchill and Miss Pemberley. Did you hear it, too?"

"Hear what?"

"The church bell at St Swithun's. Didn't you hear it?"

"Ringing again, was it?"

"No, it fell off!"

"Oh dear." Churchill considered the size and weight of a church bell for a moment. "I hope no one was hurt," she added.

A lady Churchill hadn't seen before joined them. She had grey curls tinged with mauve and wore a coat with a fur-trimmed collar. "Terrible news," she said.

"It must have been an awful racket for you, Mrs Purseglove," said Mrs Thonnings, "what with you living opposite the church."

"It was indeed. Instead of the endless ringing we've grown accustomed to, we heard an almighty thud!"

"Oh dear."

"Apparently, someone's been squashed," added Mrs Purseglove.

The ladies gasped.

"How awful!" exclaimed Churchill.

"Dreadful!" said Mrs Thonnings with a frantic shake of her head.

"Who's been squashed?" asked Mrs Crackleby.

"I can't say for sure," replied Mrs Purseglove, "but I'd hazard a guess that it was Mr Spooner."

"Who's he?" asked Churchill.

"The tower captain," replied Mrs Thonnings.

"Or ringing master," said Mrs Harris.

"He's a campanologist," added Mrs Crackleby.

"A belfry man," said Mrs Purseglove. "The only belfry man in the village after last week!"

"What happened last week?" asked Churchill.

"It's a long story," replied Mrs Purseglove, "but suffice it to say that the bells of St Swithun's may never ring again."

"Now I understand why everyone's heading down the high street, Pembers," said Churchill once they had left their group of friends behind. "They're all walking toward the church. How awful of people to go and gawp at the scene of an accident like that. Shall we go and see what's happening?"

"Gawp, you mean?"

"Oh, no. Not us! We view such incidents through the eyes of professional investigators. We have enquiring minds."

"It doesn't sound very different from gawping."

"It very much is, and a little stroll past the church won't do us any harm after all those scones. Come along, Miss Pemberley. Oswald's already got wind of something."

The little dog had started trotting on over the cobbles ahead of them, so the two ladies followed behind him.

"When Mrs Purseglove mentioned that Mr Spooner had been squashed," said Churchill, "do you think she meant he was deceased?"

"I don't think she knew. And besides, she was only guessing that it was Mr Spooner at all."

"Well, quite. I hope the poor chap makes a full recovery if he isn't deceased. Although I really don't know how one would go about making a full recovery from a church bell falling on one's head."

"It probably depends on the size of the bell. If it were the smallest one he might be all right, but if it were the biggest one…"

"It doesn't bear thinking about it, does it?"

On reaching the end of the high street, the ladies followed the narrow lane that led up to the pretty little church.

"How old would you say St Swithun's is, Pembers?"

"I think part of it is nine hundred years old."

"Good grief! Which part?"

"I'm not sure, but I know it's been added to many times over the years."

"Could the bells be nine hundred years old?"

"Oh, no. They're only likely to have been in place for two or three hundred years."

"It's no wonder they're falling off!"

A group of people had gathered beside the churchyard's kissing gate.

"It doesn't look like they're letting anybody in," commented Churchill. "That was to be expected, I suppose." She caught the attention of a youth chewing on a piece of straw "Excuse me, young man. Do you happen to know who was squashed by the church bell?"

"Old Jeremy Spooner."

"Oh dear. And is he…?"

"Yeah, 'e's dead."

"Oh dear." She turned back to Pemberley. "It's as we feared. Shall we return to the office?"

Pemberley nodded and the two ladies went on their way.

"What a way to go, Pembers," mused Churchill. "Imagine being squashed by a church bell."

"I can only hope that Mr Spooner knew nothing about it."

Chapter 2

A SQUARE-FACED LADY WITH LONG, grey hair was waiting by the door to Churchill and Pemberley's office when they returned.

"Mrs Higginbath," said Churchill nervously. "I'm quite sure we don't have any overdue library books here. Miss Pemberley, is *The Havana Heist* still within its loan period?"

"Yes."

"It's not on one of those short loans, is it?"

"No, it's a standard three-week loan."

"Good. And I can assure you, Mrs Higginbath, that Mrs Thonnings has absolutely not loaned me any of her library books recently—"

"I should hope not!" snapped the librarian.

"Is there anything else you can think of, Miss Pemberley, that we might have done to prompt Mrs Higginbath's visit to us today?"

Pemberley shook her head timorously. Oswald cowered behind her skirt.

"At ease, Mrs Churchill," said Mrs Higginbath. "For the first time ever, I'm not about to tell you off."

"Well, that's a relief. Shall we step inside?"

Mrs Higginbath made herself comfortable in the chair opposite Churchill.

"Would you like a slice of ginger and raisin cake?" Churchill asked her.

"No, thank you. I don't like the sound of that one."

"Never mind. Ginger isn't for everyone."

"It's the raisins I don't like."

"I see." Churchill began to cut the cake into slices while Pemberley made the tea.

"In fact, I really detest raisins," continued Mrs Higginbath.

"Well, fortunately for me, I'm rather a fan," replied Churchill. She placed a thick slice on her plate and licked her lips.

"I think they look like spiders with their legs cut off," added Mrs Higginbath.

Churchill felt her appetite slipping away like a crocodile sliding off a riverbank.

"Thank you for that, Mrs Higginbath. I know who to turn to whenever I need to start avoiding the good things in life." She picked up her pen and notebook. "What brings you to our little office today?"

"I never thought the day would come when I would be requesting your help, Mrs Churchill."

"Neither did I."

"Funny how circumstances bring people together, isn't it?"

Mrs Higginbath forced the corners of her mouth into an ugly grimace, which Churchill deduced was an attempt at a friendly smile.

"The truth is, I need your help with something,"

continued the librarian. "I've already asked Inspector Mappin, but he's rather busy."

"Busy not doing his job, you mean?"

"That's a little harsh, Mrs Churchill. He has a lot of work to do, and I suppose my request is something he doesn't consider to be urgent."

"What exactly is your request?"

"I've had something stolen."

"In that case, he should be taking it extremely seriously, Mrs Higginbath! Are you saying that something's been stolen and he's refusing to help?"

"He hasn't refused. He's working on it, but it's taking rather a long time."

Churchill's pen was poised over a fresh sheet of paper in her notebook. "Right, fire away, Mrs Higginbath. What is it you've had stolen?"

"It's rather valuable."

"Hence your visit today. You're quite desperate to retrieve it, no doubt."

"Yes. Very desperate, actually. I'm sure you'll be aware, Mrs Churchill, that I didn't make the decision to ask for your help lightly."

"Absolutely. But now that you *have* asked for it, I shall do what I can to help."

Pemberley brought in the tea tray and placed it on Churchill's desk. "You haven't started on the cake yet, Mrs Churchill?"

"Not yet, Miss Pemberley."

"That's not like you."

"No, it's not. Now, listen carefully. Mrs Higginbath is about to tell us what she's had stolen."

"Stolen? Golly!" Pemberley clasped her hands together and listened intently.

"I've had an ornament stolen," said Mrs Higginbath.

"An eighteenth-century figurine, to be precise. Porcelain. It depicts a courting couple."

"A courting couple? I didn't have you down as the sort of person who would own a porcelain figurine of a courting couple."

"There's a lot you don't know about me, Mrs Churchill."

"I'm sure there is. Can you please describe this figurine for me?"

"It's rather charming, actually. It depicts a young lady in flowered skirts and a tightly laced bodice sitting in a bower with a young lamb on her lap. There are flowers at her feet and her suitor is sitting on the ground with her hand in his. He's gazing at her imploringly, wearing a rather fetching pink jacket, gold breeches, white stockings and little black shoes with flowers on. Interestingly, she is also wearing little black shoes with flowers on. And both are wearing enchanting little hats."

"It sounds very charming indeed," replied Churchill, struggling to reconcile the description of the delicate ornament with the fearsome lady sitting opposite her. "And when was it stolen?"

"It must have been about a fortnight ago. It was taken from my mantelpiece while I was out posting a letter."

"I wonder, Mrs Higginbath, if you left your door open while you were out. As someone who lived in London for many years, I've always struggled to comprehend the rather rural habit of leaving one's door wide open without a second thought. I do understand that it's commonplace in these parts, however, and I can only assume that's what you did that day."

"That's exactly what I did, Mrs Churchill. How well observed of you. I've been leaving my front door open whenever I pop out to post a letter for about fifty years now, and not once has anybody strayed inside my house and taken anything. It really is a first. I presume the culprit was an opportunist. He must have been strolling along the street and noticed the open door, then decided to sidle in and help himself to something. It must have been someone who has an eye for valuable items, because he chose the most expensive ornament I own. And it isn't just the expense, of course. The item is also of great sentimental value to me."

"Did you inherit it? Or was it a gift?"

"It was a gift from a very dear friend."

"I see. And presumably you didn't see anybody walking past your home at the time the ornament was taken?"

"No. Nobody who looked out of the ordinary, in any case."

"But it may have been an ordinary-looking person who took it."

"I suppose so, but I could hardly expect it to have been one of my neighbours. It has to have been an interloper. An interloper who is very good at covering his tracks."

"You may be right, Mrs Higginbath. We'll see what we can do."

"Good golly, Pembers," said Churchill once the librarian had left. "I never thought I'd see the day when Mrs Higginbath would step inside our office and be perfectly nice to us. It made for a refreshing change, didn't it?"

"It certainly did."

"I wonder if she'll finally allow me to have a reading ticket for the library if we manage to find her porcelain figurine. That remains to be seen, I suppose. As for the gift from a dear friend, what do you make of that, Pembers?

Who do you suppose Mrs Higginbath's dear friend is… or was?"

"I've no idea. I suppose there are a few people she could almost call friends. But as for a *dear* friend, I really don't know."

Chapter 3

"HAVE YOU HEARD THE LATEST?" asked the village haberdasher as she marched into Churchill and Pemberley's office the following morning.

"No, but I'm quite sure you have, Mrs Thonnings," replied Churchill. "You always manage to hear the latest news first."

"I have connections." She tapped the side of her nose and flopped down into a chair.

"How convenient."

"Murder!"

Churchill jumped. "Where?"

"Mr Spooner was murdered!"

Churchill's mouth hung open. "With a church bell?"

"Apparently so."

"How does someone go about murdering someone with something so large and heavy. How would they even manage it?"

"Apparently, there were signs that the bell had been tampered with."

"Tampered with in such a way that it would fall on Mr Spooner when he pulled the rope?"

"Exactly that, Mrs Churchill. Is that lemon drizzle cake on your desk?"

"Yes, but we're saving it for later. I've some nice ginger and raisin cake if you'd like a slice of that instead."

"Yes, please."

Churchill opened the cake tin and took out the slice she had cut for herself the previous day. "I must say I'm rather impressed by Inspector Mappin's detective skills if he's already managed to find evidence that the bell had been tampered with." She handed the slice of cake to Mrs Thonnings.

"It was Mr Whiplark the steeple keeper who noticed it. He checks the bells every week, and he says they were fine just a few days ago. But Inspector Mappin's had him look at the bell and the bell frame in the belfry, and he reckons there were signs of tampering. I can't claim to know how bells work, but it had supposedly been interfered with in such a way that the whole thing would come down with just one tug of the rope."

"Which is exactly what happened."

"Yes! And to ensure that the job was done properly, the murderer chose to tamper with the tenor bell."

"Why's that?"

"It's the heaviest one. Weighs about ten hundredweight."

"Good grief!"

"That's half a ton," commented Pemberley.

"Is it?" responded Churchill. "I had no idea a bell could be that heavy."

"It's made quite a mess of the church tower," continued Mrs Thonnings. "It went crashing through the clock chamber, then down into the ringing chamber. That's where it struck poor old Mr Spooner, carrying him on down into the choir vestry at the bottom."

"That sounds horrendous," said Churchill.

"And that's where he was found. In the choir vestry, squashed beneath a heavy old bell."

"How barbaric. The person who carried out this murder must be a truly dreadful individual. Just think of all the other innocents who might have got themselves caught up in it!"

"Mr Spooner was innocent, too," said Pemberley.

"Well, absolutely. That goes without saying. I wonder if he was the intended target, come to think of it."

"I hope he was," said Mrs Thonnings. "Otherwise he died needlessly."

"One could argue that he died needlessly either way, Mrs Thonnings. What was Mr Spooner like?"

"Noisy," replied the haberdasher. "Very noisy."

"In what respect?"

"In every respect. For one thing, he was always ringing those church bells."

"Well, he was a belfry man."

"Yes, but he rang them far more than he needed to. Any excuse, he rang them. He made life hell for the people who live near the church."

"Who'd have thought that living next door to God's house would be hell-like."

"People were up in arms about it all," continued Mrs Thonnings. "I imagine some will be quite pleased to finally have a bit of peace and quiet."

"Are you saying that someone may have wanted to have him silenced?"

"Undoubtedly! And it wasn't just the church bell. He spoke loudly, too. He had a very loud, booming voice, and whenever he spoke he would hold his face very close to yours and shout."

"That doesn't sound very sociable."

"Maybe he was hard of hearing," suggested Pemberley.

"What do you mean?" responded Mrs Thonnings.

"Maybe he struggled to hear properly, and that's why he spoke more loudly than he needed to."

"There was nothing wrong with his hearing," replied the haberdasher. "He was just a noisy man. He had great big, thick-soled, clobbery boots he used to stomp around in. You could hear him coming from half a mile away."

"Half a mile away?"

"I'm exaggerating, of course, but you get my drift. There he was with his loud, booming voice and his great big noisy boots, shouting away first thing in the morning as he made his way to the church. Then he started ringing the bells. I'm surprised he wasn't murdered sooner, really."

"It sounds as though he made rather a nuisance of himself."

"Yes, he did! And although I'm awfully sorry that he's dead, the village will certainly be a lot quieter from now on."

"*Are* you sorry he's dead, Mrs Thonnings? You don't sound very sorry about it."

"I didn't like him, to be honest, so in that sense I'm not sorry. But it's always sad when someone dies, and it's much worse when that someone has been murdered. Even though he was noisy and we'll all be able to live in peace now, I feel very strongly that the murderer must be caught."

"Absolutely, Mrs Thonnings. Whatever we think of the victim, it's very important that the murderer is apprehended. A good detective never passes judgement or allows bias to influence her investigation."

"I couldn't agree more. Thank you for the lovely slice of cake, Mrs Churchill."

"You can have the rest if you like." Churchill picked up the cake tin and handed it to her.

"You don't want it?"

"No, you have it."

"What's wrong with it?"

"Nothing's wrong with it."

"There must be something wrong with it if you don't want it!"

"I'm not *that* obsessed with cake!"

"Really? I thought you were."

"Please accept it as a gift, Mrs Thonnings."

"Well, if you're sure."

"Consider it a thank you for the little briefing you've just given us."

"Get your stoutest walking shoes on, Pembers," said Churchill once Mrs Thonnings had left. "We need to get ourselves down to St Swithun's church."

"Do you think we can help find out who the murderer is, Mrs Churchill?"

"We've never failed in any of our previous cases, have we? Let's keep our investigations quiet, though. We don't want Mappin cottoning on to the fact that we're at all interested in this case. He'll accuse us of meddling again. We'll just make a quick, surreptitious visit to the church, and no one will ever know we were there."

"A swift sidle in, then a swift sidle out?"

"Exactly that."

Chapter 4

"I DON'T LIKE THIS CHURCHYARD," said Pemberley as the two ladies and their dog walked through the kissing gate and up the path to the church. "I keep thinking of those horrible frights we had here while we were investigating the murder of Mr Butterfork."

"That sinister sexton didn't help matters when he jumped out at us under the cover of darkness."

"Oh, don't remind me!"

"But we survived, didn't we? Come along now, Pembers. Let's see what we can find inside this church." Churchill pushed open the large, creaky door, and they stepped inside the musty-smelling porch. "Damp," she remarked. "You always know you're in a nice old church when you can smell the damp."

The porch opened out onto the left side of the nave. Sunlight streamed in through the stained-glass windows, projecting beams of colour onto the columns supporting the high, arched roof.

Oswald began investigating the pews and sniffing at the prayer cushions.

"This place is nine hundred years old, eh, Pembers?" Churchill peered up at the ancient beams.

"Some of it," replied Pemberley. "Probably just the foundations and maybe that little chapel over there. The roof truss above us is only about six hundred years old."

"What if it's riddled with woodworm?" Churchill said with a shudder. "The whole lot could come crashing down without warning!"

"It's probably been riddled with woodworm for about four hundred years. If it hasn't fallen down in all that time, it's unlikely to suddenly do so in the brief time we're standing here."

"Talking of falling down, let's go and investigate the damage to the bell tower. It's an awful thing to admit, Pembers, but I'm afraid I haven't attended this church terribly often. Do you happen to know where the choir vestry might be?"

"Just over here." Pemberley walked toward the rear of the church where there was a door in the wall behind the font. She tried the handle. "Oh dear, the door's locked. I suppose it's been locked out of respect following this terrible incident. It is where Mr Spooner was found dead, after all."

"Shame." Churchill tried the handle once more, just in case Pemberley hadn't quite turned it properly. "No, it's no use. We can't get in there. What I'd like to know is how on earth someone gets up a bell tower to begin with. Where is the way up?"

Pemberley glanced around. "There must be a door that leads to it somewhere."

"Over here, perhaps?" Churchill strode over to a smaller door, which was arched and had elaborate iron hinges. She tried the handle and it opened onto a spiral staircase made of stone. "This must be the way up,

Pembers. I must say it looks rather snug. It's a good thing I have a torch in my handbag."

As Churchill switched on her torch and examined the stone steps, Oswald darted around her and scampered up the staircase.

"Did he have something in his mouth just then?" asked Churchill.

"I think it was a prayer cushion."

"Oh, good grief!"

"He won't damage it, if that's what you're worried about, Mrs Churchill. He just likes to carry things about in his mouth sometimes."

"Right, well we need to get up this staircase so we can have a good look at the bell tower and retrieve that prayer cushion."

"We?"

"Yes. Come along, Pembers."

"Oh no, Mrs Churchill. I couldn't possibly go up that old spiral staircase. It's too narrow and dingy and twisty-turny. The very thought of it gives me the heebie-jeebies."

Churchill examined the staircase again. "It's certainly narrow, I'll give you that. People were smaller in the olden days, weren't they? Your dog seems to have been quite happy to go up there, though. That should reassure you."

"There's nothing I hate more than old stone staircases."

"I refuse to believe that, Pembers. Surely there are worse things."

"I can't think of any just at this moment."

"Very well. You wait here and I shall go up the bell tower."

"Are you sure, Mrs Churchill? It's very high up."

"We need to examine the murder scene, Pembers, and

with the door to the choir thingy locked, climbing the bell tower is our only other option. Now, stop fretting and keep a lookout. If you see Mappin knocking about, give a loud whistle and I'll hurry back down again." Churchill squeezed herself through the little doorway.

"Oh, do be careful, Mrs Churchill!"

"I'm always careful."

Churchill tackled the first few steps with great gusto. After a short while, however, she grew tired of the way the steps spiralled so sharply to the right. Climbing them was rather dizzying, and it wasn't long before she found herself quite out of breath.

She began to wonder whether Pemberley had been right. *Is it really necessary to climb the bell tower?* she asked herself. Churchill paused for a moment and reasoned that she would look rather foolish returning to her assistant when so little time had elapsed. Having set her mind on climbing the staircase, there was nothing for it but to continue her ascent.

A small landing with a little window and doorway provided some relief. Churchill peered out of the open window to see the roof sloping down to the churchyard.

"I must be about fifty feet up," she said to herself. She tried the door handle, which opened into a small room with whitewashed walls. Several ropes were looped up out of reach above her, and a large hole in the floor was aligned with a similar one in the ceiling.

"Golly," said Churchill, open-mouthed as she edged cautiously into the room.

Splintered floorboards and beams jutted over the gap in the floor. Churchill's heart began to thud and she felt wary of getting too close. Above her, more broken planks of wood hung precariously from the damaged roof. "This is the bell-ringing chamber," she said to herself. "Mrs Thonnings said the bell crashed through the clock chamber first, then the bell-ringing chamber and down into the choir vestry below." The senior detective gave the damage one final look before returning to the spiral staircase with a shudder.

After a little more climbing, Churchill's ankles began to ache and her thighs burned. Puffing heavily, she passed the door that could only lead into the damaged clock chamber. Continuing on, she managed the final few steps that led to an arched doorway at the very top.

"The belfry," she wheezed, barely finding the breath to speak. Pushing open the door, she continued up a few narrow wooden steps, which brought her alongside the church bells.

Daylight filtered in through the slatted louvre windows in each wall. The dull bronze bells hung next to several large wooden cartwheels. Attached to the wheels were ropes, which Churchill surmised fed down into the ringing chamber below.

"I see how it works now," she said to herself proudly. "The bell-ringer pulls on the rope, which pulls on the wheel, which turns the bell and makes it clang."

She gave a satisfied nod and counted the bells. There were seven in all. Then she spotted the gap where the fallen bell had once hung. Its metal frame remained in place, but she could see where the missing bolts should have been.

She shuddered again. "Poor Mr Spooner didn't stand a chance. Who came up here and caused this terrible mischief?"

. . .

Churchill's descent was easier than her climb, but she felt rather light-headed by the time she finally stumbled back out into the nave of the church.

"How did you get on, Mrs Churchill?"

"It was very enlightening. Oh dear, I need to sit down for a moment. Let's take a pew. All I can see is those spiral steps going down and round, down and round…"

Once Pemberley had led her employer over to one of the pews, Churchill told her what she had seen.

"A great deal of planning went into this murder, Pembers," she said. "Someone climbed that spiral staircase with all the tools they needed to loosen that bell. And somehow they managed it without anybody noticing."

"Not even the steeple keeper."

"Exactly. Not even him."

"Where's Oswald?" asked Pemberley.

"Oh, he'll be around here somewhere." Churchill glanced about, realising she hadn't encountered the dog since he had scampered up the staircase ahead of her. "I assumed he'd already come back down. Did he not?"

"No," replied Pemberley. "I thought he was with you. Oh, heavens! Where's he got to?"

"He couldn't have got into the bell-ringing chamber or the belfry because I had to open doors to get inside them, and I didn't even open the door for the clock chamber. All he could have done was climb the staircase and come back down again. He must have done so without you noticing."

"I'm sure I would have noticed him. And even if I hadn't, he'd be running about down here by now."

"Indeed he would. I didn't even see the prayer cushion anywhere. They sometimes lose interest in such things and leave them in haphazard places, don't they?"

"Oswald!" Pemberley called out, her voice echoing around the nave. "Oswald!"

"Goodness, that's quite deafening, Pembers," commented Churchill. "The acoustics in this place are splendid, aren't they?"

"Never mind the acoustics," retorted Pemberley as she scrambled to her feet. "I need to find Oswald!"

As Pemberley scurried around the pews, Churchill thought about the staircase. *Was there anywhere the dog could have hidden himself away?* She knew he couldn't have entered the bell-ringing chamber or the belfry, but there had been a window opposite the door to the bell-ringing chamber, and Churchill felt sure it had been open. Her heart leapt up into her throat.

"Let's have a look for him outside," she said as calmly as possible, rising to her feet.

"Why would he be outside?" replied Pemberley. "He can't have got outside. We closed the door behind us."

"Well… I did pass an open window up there," replied Churchill.

"An *open window* in the tower?" A look of horror spread across Pemberley's face. "Could he have got through it?"

"Anything's possible."

"*Oswald!*" shrieked Pemberley as she headed for the main door.

Churchill did her best to trot after her assistant, but she could already feel her legs beginning to seize up after the bell-tower climb.

"Which window was it?" asked Pemberley frantically once the two ladies were out in the churchyard.

"That one there." Churchill pointed up at the tower.

"At the very top?"

"No, not at the top. That's the belfry. It's that one there, overlooking the roof. Uh oh… I think I see him now. Do you?"

High up on the ridge of the church roof was the black

silhouette of a scruffy little dog, stumbling along. A large object hung from his mouth.

"Has he still got that prayer cushion?"

"It looks like it. Oh, help, Mrs Churchill! How are we ever going to get him down?"

Chapter 5

"Would you care to explain, Mrs Churchill, how your dog came to be stuck on the roof of St Swithun's church?"

"He's not *my* dog, Inspector Mappin. He's Miss Pemberley's dog. And no, I can't explain it at all."

The bushy-whiskered inspector scowled and noted something down in his book. Churchill looked up to see a fireman gingerly making his way along the ridge of the roof and attempting to coax the dog toward him.

"Oh, do be careful!" Pemberley cried out. "He's going to fall and break his neck, I just know it!"

"What's he got in his mouth?" the inspector asked Churchill.

"A prayer cushion."

He made another note. "A reimbursement will be required for that."

"He won't damage it."

"We'll have to see about that. Interesting, don't you think, Mrs Churchill, that your dog—"

"*Miss Pemberley's* dog."

"That Miss Pemberley's dog has ended up in a location where it was recently confirmed that a murder had taken place. You weren't by any chance snooping about the place, were you?"

"Snooping about, Inspector? What do you take us for? Anyway, we're being ably assisted by the fire brigade at the minute. I can't see why it's a matter for the police at all."

"The incident has created quite the drama in the village," Inspector Mappin replied, glancing around at the small crowd that had gathered.

"Drama or no drama, Inspector, it is not a police matter."

"Oh, but I think it is a police matter, because the only way that dog could have got up onto the roof would be via the window in the bell tower. The very same tower that just happens to be the scene of a recent crime. That's why you're here, isn't it?"

Churchill gave an uneasy laugh. "Do I look like someone who likes to go squeezing herself through small doors and clambering up seventy steps of a narrow spiral staircase?"

"You seem very au fait with the layout of the bell tower for someone who has supposedly never been inside it," he responded.

"All right, all right, I admit it. But what else did you expect? I heard the awful news that Mr Spooner's death was being treated as murder and, as Miss Pemberley and I were walking past the church at the time, we thought that it would be helpful if we came and had a little look for ourselves. After all, we're rather good at solving these kinds of cases, Inspector. You might actually need a little help."

"I can assure you, Mrs Churchill, that I do not require any help with this case. My usual constable helpers from

Bulchford will be helping with the investigation, and I'll also have Chief Inspector Llewellyn-Dalrymple from Dorchester looking in from time to time."

"Lucky you."

"I will not be needing the assistance of two old ladies."

"If you say so, Inspector."

"I advise you to not waste any of your time on this case, Mrs Churchill. I realise you're quite determined to set yourself up as a private detective, but there are many other matters a private detective could spend her time working on in this village. There's no need for you to go around interfering with an ongoing police investigation. In fact, your assistance, as you describe it, is a great hindrance to us. Look at all the time the fire brigade here have wasted in retrieving your dog. It's safe to say that he wouldn't have been up on the roof at all if you hadn't been snooping around the church."

"I really wish you wouldn't describe it as *snooping*, Inspector. Miss Pemberley and I have every right to visit our local church, and I'm sure the vicar would have no objection at all."

"I'm sure he would have an objection if your visit resulted in your dog scrambling about on his rooftop with a fireman in pursuit. Both are in danger of either dislodging a roof tile or slipping off altogether. Let's hope he doesn't come to any harm for your sake, Mrs Churchill."

"I'm sure Oswald will be fine."

"I was referring to the fireman."

"I'm extremely grateful for the help of the fire brigade. They're ever so useful at times like this."

"Yes, they are. Let's just hope there isn't a fire while they're busy trying to rescue your wayward dog."

The fireman had managed to get quite close to

Oswald, but the little dog seemed to think he wanted to play. In his excitement he dropped the prayer cushion, which tumbled down the steep roof, bounced off the guttering and landed with a soft thud on top of an ornate tomb.

Chapter 6

"So much for a quiet sidle in and out of the church, Pembers," said Churchill as the two ladies walked up the hill to the vicarage. "Most of the village knows I went up the bell tower now; not least of all, Inspector Mappin. He's the very last person we wanted to hear about our visit, and now he's accusing us of snooping again. Typical!"

"I'm sure the vicar will be much more forgiving," replied Pemberley, carrying Oswald in her arms.

"Given the fact that forgiveness is one of the basic tenets of Christianity, Pembers, I should fervently hope so. He wouldn't be much of a vicar if he couldn't forgive us, would he?"

"I do hope he'll be grateful for my offer of a new prayer cushion."

"Are you sure you want to set about stitching one of those? It'll take ages. You could probably just buy one from somewhere."

"I don't want to *buy* one, Mrs Churchill. I want to *make* one. I'll visit Mrs Thonnings later today to pick up some supplies."

. . .

An apple-cheeked maid at the vicarage showed the two ladies into the drawing room.

"I'll tell the vicar yer 'ere," she said as she left the room.

Churchill glanced around her. "We were last in this place for the Vicarage Christmas Party, Pembers. Do you remember?"

"How could I forget? That was the night of the dreadful murder of Mr Donkin."

"Yes. That subdued the celebrations a little. Oh, hello, Vicar. How are you?"

A tall, large-nosed man with thin wisps of white hair and watery grey eyes entered the room. "Very well, thank you, Mrs Churchill. Miss Pemberley. Do take a seat."

The two ladies sat themselves down on a floral settee.

"First of all, Vicar, Miss Pemberley and I would like to apologise for the way Miss Pemberley's dog has been running about on the church roof," said Churchill.

"Ah, yes. I heard about that. That's the fellow there, is it? Is he all right?"

"He's perfectly well and none the worse for his ordeal."

"Jolly good."

"I'd like to stitch a new prayer cushion, Vicar," said Pemberley, "to replace the one that was hurled from the roof and landed on the tomb of Sir Ronald Eversley."

"That's very kind of you, Miss Pemberley. We already have a fair few, to be honest with you. In fact, I often find myself tripping over them in church. People seem to scatter them all over the place during Communion. I don't know how they manage it!"

"I'd like to make one all the same."

"Very well. I look forward to seeing it."

"We would also like to express our condolences to you, Vicar," said Churchill, "following the death of your esteemed belfry man, Mr Spooner."

"Thank you, Mrs Churchill. It's been a very sad time indeed."

"I can't even begin to think who might have committed such a despicable act."

"Me neither."

"And to cause such terrible damage to the church at the same time!"

"Indeed, indeed." The vicar wiped his brow. "It really is a terrible travesty all round. An astonishing amount of damage and the death of an innocent man. There's just no explanation for tragedies like this."

"It makes you wonder whether there really is a God after all," said Pemberley.

"Miss Pemberley!" exclaimed Churchill. "You mustn't say such things; especially in the presence of the reverend, and in his own home as well!"

He shook his head wearily. "Miss Pemberley makes a valid point," he said. "It's times like these that sorely test one's faith. 'My God, my God, why hast thou forsaken me?'"

"Indeed. Well, poor Mr Spooner was very much forsaken, and we need to find out who was responsible."

"We certainly do. What sort of a devil commits murder in a church? I hope he'll be hung, drawn and quartered when he's caught."

"I don't think that particular form of punishment has been carried out within the British Isles for a few hundred years, Vicar."

"Then it should be brought back! This was an abominable thing to do; vindictive and malevolent. And the level of planning that went into it also bothers me. To think that the culprit was up there loosening the bolts of the tenor bell in the full knowledge that when the next bell-ringer pulled the rope the whole thing would come crashing down on him! Such a sinister, premeditated act."

"Have you any idea when the bolts were loosened?" asked Churchill.

"Some time during the previous night, I think. We all heard the almighty clang at around ten o'clock when Jeremy Spooner pulled the bell rope in the morning. He'd rung the bell without any trouble at all at seven o'clock the previous evening. I can only imagine that the culprit somehow gained access to the church overnight."

"To the best of your knowledge, Vicar, did anybody enter the church during that time?"

"The usual bell-ringing practice was cancelled, so it was only Mr Spooner in there ringing the bells."

"On his own?"

"Yes. It doesn't sound quite the same with just one bell-ringer. There are eight bells, so eight people are needed to ring them properly. Jeremy was about to begin the process of assembling a new bell-ringing team."

"Do you know what time he left the church?"

"The sexton locked the door at eight o'clock, so Jeremy had obviously left by then."

"The church is locked at night, is it?"

"Yes."

"Did the murderer break in, then?"

"No, he must have unlocked the door."

"You think he had a key?"

"Yes."

"Well, that should narrow down the list of suspects!" said Churchill with a grin. "How many parishioners have a key to the church?"

"Lots of them do."

Her heart sank. "Really?"

"Yes. Perhaps I'm a foolish old man, but I've been known to hand keys out rather frequently in the past."

"Why did you do that?"

"There was always someone who needed to go in there after the sexton had locked up – to polish the brass or change the altar cloth or something or other. The church is unlocked all day, but you know how it is. People always seem to want to do these things after it's locked up. Over the years I've allowed various people to have their own key. There must be lots in circulation now."

"In that case, it wouldn't be too difficult to get hold of a key if one were to ask around for one?"

"No. I know it wasn't very sensible of me, but I really didn't expect anyone to commit a murder inside my church."

"Well, no one could have expected that." Churchill sighed and glanced over at the doorway, hoping the apple-cheeked maid might reappear with some refreshments. Then she turned back to the vicar. "There had been a falling out among the bell-ringers, I hear."

"Yes. There was a bit of bother last week... to the effect that they all left."

"Do you know why?"

"They visited me here and tried to explain it all to me, but everyone was rather hot under the collar, so I struggled to keep track of it. The long and the short of it was that Jeremy had annoyed them all in some way or another, and they no longer wanted any part in it. They've all gone off to join the bell-ringers in South Bungerly, apparently, which is a great shame. They've only got six bells over there at St Baldred's, so there'll be a good deal of scrapping over them now." He shook his head. "I'm sure it could all have been avoided with a bit of sensible discussion. I can't understand this hot-headed approach everybody seems so intent on these days."

"It would be helpful to speak to the disgruntled bell-ringers," said Churchill. "Would you mind giving us their names?"

"If you really want to understand what the fuss was about, Mr Whiplark is your man. He's the steeple keeper, and he appeared to me to be very much the ringleader."

"The bell-ringer ringleader? That has a certain ring to it."

Pemberley chuckled.

"I'm sorry?" responded the vicar.

"Just a feeble attempt at a little joke," Churchill said sheepishly. "Where might we find Mr Whiplark?"

"I believe his caravan is currently parked on Farmer Drumhead's farm."

Chapter 7

"BEFORE YOU GO SUGGESTIN' anythin', it weren't me what done it!"

Mr Whiplark was a small, lean man with a long grey beard that almost reached down to his navel. He wore a flat cap, spectacles and a brown leather waistcoat, and he stood outside his Romany caravan with his arms folded. A thick-set carthorse with languid eyes grazed calmly nearby, seemingly oblivious to its owner's wrath.

"Everyone reckons I done it!" he continued. "I were the steeple keeper, weren't I? I'm the one what looked after them bells. They're sayin' I'm the only one what could've loosened them bolts! Well, it weren't me, I tell yer, and I'll defend meself even if it kills me!"

"Golly!" responded Churchill. "I'm quite sure it won't come to that, Mr Whiplark. As I've just explained, my assistant Miss Pemberley and I are merely interested in finding out a little more about the disagreement you had with the late Mr Jeremy Spooner."

"It weren't me!" He sniffed. "Are yers 'elpin' the police or summat?"

"No, not at all. We're private detectives, with, I hasten to add, reasonably good form at solving murders."

"Are yer now?" He cocked his head to one side and refolded his arms. "Well, if yer any good at solvin' these things, yer'll know it weren't me!"

"Indeed, Mr Whiplark. Now, could you tell me why you fell out with Mr Spooner?"

"Not without the others. I ain't talkin' to yer without the other bell-ringers 'ere. Otherwise yer'll think it were just me what fell out wiv 'im, and it weren't. It were all of us."

"I'd be delighted to speak to your fellow bell-ringers, Mr Whiplark. Shall we arrange a little meeting?"

"Yeah." He gave a conciliatory nod. "I'll get 'em together and we'll have a talk wiv yer, Miss Churchley."

"*Churchill.*"

"You spoken to old Purseglove yet?"

"Mrs Purseglove who lives opposite the church?"

"Yer need to speak to 'er 'usband."

"*Mr* Purseglove?"

"Yeah. If anyone done it, it were 'im."

"That was an interesting suggestion from Mr Whiplark," said Churchill as the two ladies left the farm and walked back toward the village. "Do you think he genuinely suspects Mr Purseglove? Or was it merely an attempt to deflect attention away from himself?"

"There may be something in it. Mrs Purseglove seemed to know a good deal about the incident quite early on."

"That's right, she did! She told us it was Mr Spooner who had been crushed by the church bell before anything was confirmed by the police or the local newspaper."

"The Pursegloves live opposite the church, so that probably shouldn't come as a surprise."

"We need to determine whether she found out through sheer nosiness or through some sort of direct involvement, Pembers."

A short walk later, the two ladies and their dog found themselves standing beside a little row of cottages opposite the church.

"Which one belongs to the Pursegloves, Pembers?"

"I don't know."

"Oh, well. Let's try the first one here." She strode up to the little blue door of the first cottage and gave a firm knock.

It opened to reveal a small lady whose eyes were magnified by her thick spectacles.

Churchill introduced herself, then asked, "Would you mind telling us where Mr and Mrs Purseglove live?"

"Oh, them. They're next door."

"Thank you. I don't suppose you know much about the tragic incident at the church the other day, do you?"

"Only that it was poor Mr Spooner. Awfully sad. I used to enjoy listening to those church bells. It's very quiet without them."

"I imagine it is. Did you know Mr Spooner?"

"I knew he was Mr Spooner, but that's all I knew. I never actually spoke to him."

"I see."

"Mr Purseglove next door used to get very het up about the church bells. Said they were too noisy. He'll be extremely pleased that Mr Spooner is dead and can't ring them anymore."

"Will he indeed? How very interesting. Thank you for your help, Mrs…?"

"Mrs Rumble."

Mr Purseglove was a puffy-faced man with small, beady eyes and a scruffy cardigan. He invited the two ladies into his cramped front room, which was cluttered with books and old newspapers.

"You're here to ask me about Spooner, are you?" He removed a newspaper from the sagging settee and gestured for the two ladies to sit.

"That's right, Mr Purseglove. We hear that you became very annoyed by the ringing of the bells."

"Who didn't get annoyed by them?"

"Mrs Rumble next door, apparently. She's just told us she liked the church bells."

"Ha! That's what she told you, but I've heard some very fruity language coming from her garden when it was warm and sunny, but the bells were too loud for her to sit out."

"Really? I can't imagine Mrs Rumble ever using fruity language."

"Well, there you go. She probably wanted to show you her best side."

"Yes, she probably did. But back to yourself, Mr Purseglove. Did you know Mr Spooner well?"

"Not as a friend, but I spoke to him plenty of times about the ringing of those darned bells."

"The bells rang a lot, did they?"

"An awful lot, yes. And it was the hour at which they rang them! Seven o'clock on a Sunday morning!" He shook his head. "I know it's the Sabbath and so on, but can't a chap get a bit of peace before he has to go to church?"

"Seven o'clock on a Sunday does seem rather early."

"Exactly, Mrs Churchill. I'm pleased you agree. Spooner was an early riser, and the first thing he used to do when he got up was gather his team together and ring those infernal bells. Just the other week I marched up into that ringing chamber and tore a strip off him. I even threatened to tie that accursed bell rope around his neck."

"Cripes!"

"And the threat worked for a bit. The bells remained quiet for the rest of the day. But knock me down with a feather if he wasn't back there the next day, hanging off his rope again and clanging away without a care in the world! Nothing could stop the man for long."

"Did you speak to the vicar about it?"

"Did I speak to the vicar about it? All the time! I realise he's the shepherd of our flock and all the rest of it, but he's also a wet fish. He kept saying he'd have a word with Spooner and the other bell-ringers, but it never came to anything. I think he was frightened of him. Don't ask me why, because there was nothing frightening about Spooner whatsoever, but there you have it. And now it's all come to an end. He got what was coming to him."

"Goodness. Do you really think Mr Spooner deserved to be murdered for the noise he was making?"

"I'm afraid so, Mrs Churchill. There's only so much us villagers can take."

"Has Inspector Mappin spoken to you yet?"

"No. Why would he?"

"Well, as he's investigating this case, he'll probably be drawing up a list of suspects. I hope you don't mind me saying so, Mr Purseglove, but you appear to have had rather a strong motive for murdering Mr Spooner. Especially given that you threatened to tie the bell rope around his neck."

"Yes, but he knew I didn't mean anything by it!" He chuckled, seemingly amused by his own threat. "There's no need for the inspector to speak to me. He can if he wants to, I have nothing to hide, but I'm not going to pretend to him or you, Mrs Churchill, that I ever liked the fellow. If I were the murderer, I'd pretend to, wouldn't I?"

"I don't know, Mr Purseglove. Have you any idea who might have tampered with the bell and murdered Mr Spooner?"

"It will have been someone local, that's for sure. They must have been fed up with the noise, just as I was. They'll have climbed up the bell tower and loosened the bolts. Then when he pulled on that bell rope... Dong! The whole thing came crashing down on top of him. It must have been someone local, Mrs Churchill."

Chapter 8

"I'M DESPERATELY in need of a little something, Pembers," said Churchill as the two ladies walked up the high street to their office. "So far we've visited the vicar, Mrs Rumble and Mr Purseglove, and none of them saw fit to furnish us with any refreshments! What is this world coming to?"

"Don't worry, Mrs Churchill. We'll soon be back at the office, where a nice batch of jam tarts awaits us."

"Oh, goody." Churchill felt her mouth begin to water. "I can't comprehend doing anything else today until I've eaten at least three. In fact, my legs are beginning to feel so weak that I'll be lucky if I make it back to the office at all."

"Don't give up, Mrs Churchill. You can do it."

"Thank you for the encouragement. It means a lot to me."

"Detective work is truly exhausting."

"It certainly is. And when one has had to go without any sort of provision for hours on end it becomes almost unbearable."

"Oh, look! It's Mrs Higginbath again."

A feeling of panic erupted in Churchill's chest. "Where? Has she seen us yet? Can we escape?"

"I'm afraid not."

The square-faced, grey-haired lady had positioned herself on the cobbled street in front of them.

"Golly! You startled me, Mrs Higginbath!" exclaimed Churchill. "Where did you spring from?"

"How are you getting on with finding my stolen figurine?"

Churchill sighed, feeling a strong sense of resentment toward the woman standing between her and the jam tarts. "I'm afraid we haven't made any inquiries yet. We've been a little distracted by this terrible murder."

The librarian rolled her eyes. "I suppose that'll completely take over now, won't it? All the other important investigations will be forgotten about. That was why I turned to you in the first place, Mrs Churchill, after Inspector Mappin failed to act on this awful theft."

"We haven't forgotten about it, Mrs Higginbath. I can assure you that we shall devote plenty of time to your figurine, but I'm afraid we're still in the early stages of our investigation."

"Early stages? I very much doubt you've even begun the first stage, Mrs Churchill."

"Oh, but we very much *have* started. There's an awful lot that goes on behind the scenes when one is investigating a case, you know. We don't tell our clients every single aspect because it would only bore them, but there's a great deal of preparatory work to do, isn't there, Miss Pemberley?"

Pemberley nodded.

"All right, then," responded the librarian. "I shall return to check up on you soon."

"We look forward to it immensely, Mrs Higginbath."

. . .

"I suppose we'd better do a bit of work on Mrs Higginbath's stolen figurine," said Churchill as she sat back in her chair, wiping the jam tart crumbs from her mouth with her handkerchief.

"She'll be very cross with us if we don't." Pemberley poured out the tea and handed Churchill a cup.

"Thank you, Pembers. A good cup of tea sorts everything out, doesn't it?"

"Not everything."

"But most things."

"Not even most things."

"Right, well I don't have time to get embroiled in an argument like that at this very moment. Now, let's consider the potential motive of the person who took Mrs Higginbath's figurine. Do you think the culprit was a collector of eighteenth-century porcelain ornaments? Or was it someone who just wanted to make a bit of easy money?"

"I think it's more likely to have been the latter. It must have been an opportunist, because he happened to see that her door had been left open. He must have stepped in, seen the ornament on the mantlepiece and made off with it."

"Let's assume, then, that the culprit took the ornament because he wanted to make a bit of money. Where would he have taken it to do so?"

"Mr Sawyer the pawnbroker, perhaps? Or maybe he tried to sell it at a pub?"

"This is good thinking, Pembers. I like this." Churchill helped herself to another jam tart. "Let's make the pawnbroker's our next port of call. Have you ever been in there?"

"Not the one in Compton Poppleford. I've visited pawnbrokers in the past, though."

"Oh dear, Pembers. I had no idea you'd fallen on such hard times."

"Oh, it wasn't me. It was the lady of international travel I worked for. She wasn't very good at managing her finances, you see. She either had a lot of money or no money at all. Now and again I'd be sent off to pawn a piece of her jewellery. She was always able to buy it back in the end."

"All's well that ends well. Where's the pawnbroker in Compton Poppleford?"

"In the smelly alleyway next to the town hall."

"Oh, that place." Churchill wrinkled her nose. "I started walking down it once but had to turn back. Is that really where we need to go?"

"I'm afraid so."

A short while later, Churchill and Pemberley held their noses as they walked along the narrow, smelly alleyway. Oswald sniffed enthusiastically at curious little doorways and gobbled up the remnants of a discarded sandwich.

The distinctive sign of three bronze balls signalled the location of the pawnbroker's shop. Several hand-painted notices in the window listed the items that could be bought and sold there.

"We buy old gold, diamonds, watches and silver," Pemberley read aloud, her voice pitching a little higher through her pinched nose.

"Looks like we've found the right place," responded Churchill.

"Fishing rods, luggage, field glasses, cameras..." continued Pemberley.

"Very good. Shall we step inside?"

"Loans made on furs, sporting goods and instruments."

"Yes, I get the idea, Pembers. Let's go in and ask Mr Sawyer whether anyone's offered him a porcelain figurine."

Mr Sawyer was a broad man with oiled hair. He wore a wide-striped suit with a burgundy and gold cravat that matched the handkerchief in his top pocket.

"Good afternoon, ladies!" he said with a toothy grin. "And what a lovely afternoon it is. Are you buying or selling?"

"Neither," responded Churchill.

His face fell. "How can I help you, then?"

"I'm Mrs Churchill and this is Miss Pemberley. We're private detectives on the lookout for a porcelain figurine. We were wondering if anybody had offered you such an item to buy?"

"A porcelain figurine? What does it look like?"

"It's of a courting couple."

He gave another broad grin. "Courting, eh? That's the sort of ornament it is, is it?"

"It's very modest and genteel," replied Churchill haughtily, "and unlikely to be the sort of figurine you have in mind, Mr Sawyer."

"That's a shame. Very well, then. Give me a full description."

"Well, neither my assistant nor I have actually seen it, but we're told that it features a young lady with a lamb on her lap."

"She's sitting in a bower," said Pemberley.

"And the suitor is kneeling and holding her hand. He's wearing a… What was the colour of his jacket, Miss Pemberley?"

"Pink."

"That's right. A pink jacket."

"And gold breeches," added Pemberley.

"Didn't Mrs Higginbath mention that there were flowers on their shoes?"

"Yes, flowers on their shoes. And enchanting little hats."

"That's right! They're both wearing enchanting little hats, Mr Sawyer. Do you recall seeing it?"

"No."

"No one's been in to offer you such an item for sale?"

"Nope. Do you have a photograph of it?"

"Now, that would have been a very good idea. Why didn't we ask Mrs Higginbath for a photograph of it, Miss Pemberley?"

"I don't know."

"I don't know either. But I do know that it would make our job a little easier if we had one. We must ask Mrs Higginbath if she has a photograph of it."

"You should always take a photograph of valuable items," said the pawnbroker. "You never know when someone's going to nab them, and it makes life a lot easier for the police to look for things. This courting couple figurine... Has it been stolen, by any chance?"

"Unfortunately, it has."

"I couldn't help but notice that you mentioned the name Mrs Higginbath." He shuddered. "That's the librarian woman, isn't it?"

"It is indeed, Mr Sawyer."

"I wouldn't fancy getting myself on the wrong side of her," he said. "Whoever's nabbed it'll be in trouble when she discovers who it was."

"Indeed they will. Any idea where the thief might have taken the figurine?"

"I'd have given him short shrift if he'd brought it in here," he replied. "I don't take stolen items, me."

"But how do you know whether something's stolen or not?"

"I just know." He tapped the side of his head with a thick finger. "I've got intuition."

"That makes two of us, Mr Sawyer. I like to pride myself on my own intuition."

"Good for you, Mrs Churchill."

"Any idea where someone might try to sell stolen goods here in Compton Poppleford, Mr Sawyer?"

"No!" He fastened one of his jacket buttons. "Why would you ask me that? I won't have anything to do with stolen goods! But I suppose if you were to stop the average person on the high street and ask them the same question, they'd probably say the Wagon and Carrot."

"The public house?"

He nodded. "A porcelain figurine would probably sell quite well in there. The Pig and Scythe is usually the place to sell cheaper items: boots, spades, cattle prods… that sort of thing. But the Wagon and Carrot is more your market for fancy ornaments and perhaps a bit of nice jewellery…" He stopped himself and scratched at his ear. "Not that I ever visit either establishment, of course."

"Of course not."

Chapter 9

"Golly, Pembers, have you bought anything nice?" asked Churchill the following morning as Pemberley walked into the office with an overloaded shopping basket.

Oswald trotted in behind her and greeted Churchill by pushing his wet nose into her hand.

"I'm just keeping Mrs Thonnings's haberdashery shop in business," said Pemberley as she hauled her shopping basket onto her desk.

"Someone's got to."

"I've bought everything I need to make the replacement prayer cushion."

"Are you really going to find the time to do that? Just buy one! Or don't even bother at all. The vicar didn't seem too upset about the loss of the last one. Didn't he grumble about tripping over them at Communion?"

"It's no use telling me that after I've just spent a fortune at Mrs Thonnings's shop, Mrs Churchill. And anyhow, I want to make a prayer cushion. I've never made one before."

"Very well, if you insist. But we have some very busy

days ahead of us, Pembers. I don't want this prayer cushion becoming a distraction."

"You won't even know I'm working on it."

"Jolly good. Now, let's make some tea and discuss our work. Did you happen to stop by the bakery on your way back from Mrs Thonnings's shop?"

"Yes." Pemberley pulled a paper bag out of her shopping basket. "Cherry buns."

"Tremendous! Sometimes I feel sure you can read my mind, Pembers. I very much felt that today was a cherry bun day during my walk here this morning. Once we've had our refreshments, we'll need to go and speak to Mrs Spooner."

"Surely she won't want to talk to us. Her husband's just been murdered!"

"I realise that, Pembers. We'll have to be tactful."

"Tactful won't be enough, Mrs Churchill. I think we should leave her be for the time being."

"But how are we ever going to draw up a list of suspects if we can't speak to Jeremy Spooner's wife?"

"We're not officially supposed to be working on this case."

"We're rarely supposed to be working on any of these cases. But look how many we've solved, regardless of the fact! I'm sure you'd agree that we need to speak to Mrs Spooner somehow, and I have no doubt that we can do it extremely carefully. We'll be a lot more diplomatic than that fool, Mappin."

"I still don't like the idea."

"How much do you know about her?"

"Not very much, although I often see her at the market. We could accidentally bump into her there, I suppose. If she's feeling brave enough to go shopping after such a terrible tragedy, that is."

"That sounds like a plan. Market day is today, isn't it?"

"Yes."

"Then what are we waiting for?"

"Tea and cherry buns?"

"Oh yes, those. Let's see to them quickly and then be on our way."

A little later, the two ladies and their dog found themselves mingling with the market-day crowd.

"Strawberries! Penny a punnet!" shouted a short, wide man wearing a grubby apron and a flat cap.

"That's not bad," said Churchill, eyeing the colourful fruit and vegetables on his stall.

"Tea towels!" hollered a woman in a garish headscarf. "Three for sixpence!"

"That's quite good, too. I should visit the market more often."

"There she is," whispered Pemberley.

"Who?"

"Mrs Spooner. The lady we came here looking for."

"Oh yes, silly me. I was busy thinking about tea towels. Where is she?"

"Just over there by the pots and pans stall. She's the one dressed entirely in black."

"As one would expect."

"She's looking at a saucepan."

"Fancy buying a new saucepan when your husband has only just been murdered. Rather odd, don't you think?"

"Maybe she's not really intending to buy it. Perhaps she's come down to the market because that's her usual habit, and she's just absentmindedly looking at things, all the while consumed with grief."

"Yes, I imagine she felt the need to get out of the

house. Perhaps I shouldn't be too quick to judge. Let's go and speak to her."

"We are going to be tactful, aren't we?"

"Of course, Pembers. I can be as courteous as a curate's cat. Just you see."

Churchill and Pemberley walked over to where Mrs Spooner was sadly examining a pan lid.

"Oh look, Miss Pemberley. They have some rather nice colanders here," announced Churchill in a forced tone. "Aren't you on the lookout for a new colander?"

"No. What made you think that, Mrs Churchill?"

Churchill lowered her voice. "I know you're not really looking for a new colander, Pembers," she hissed. "It's just a conversation piece, see? We want Mrs Spooner to overhear us so she doesn't think we've purposely walked over here to speak to her."

"Oh, I see what you mean," whispered Pemberley in reply. Then she raised her voice. "Yes, these colanders look good. It was only yesterday that I was saying how badly I needed a new one, wasn't it, Mrs Churchill?"

"It was, Miss Pemberley. And now here we are."

"After a new colander, are you, madam?" asked the rodent-faced man behind the stall. "We've some gooduns 'ere."

"I'm just doing a little research on the price of colanders," replied Pemberley quickly. "I wasn't intending to buy one today."

"Oh, right," he replied sullenly. "Well, if you ain't planning on buyin' nothin', p'raps you could make a bitta space for thems who are."

"But we *might* buy something," said Churchill, attempting to placate him. "It all depends on whether we find a colander here that looks suitable."

"Are you goin' to buy summat?" replied the market

trader, "or are you not goin' to buy summat? 'Cause I don't want you cloggin' up my stall and gettin' in the way of me other customers, who do intend on buyin' summat from me this morning."

"We're not clogging up your stall!" protested Churchill. "We have a genuine interest in buying a colander if you have the right one. Perhaps you can advise us on which colander might be best."

"What size do you want?"

"We don't know yet. Miss Pemberley, what size do you want?"

"I don't know."

"'Ow big's yer saucepan?" asked the market trader.

"I only have small saucepans," replied Pemberley. "It's only me at home. And the dog, of course, but he doesn't have much need for a saucepan."

"If yer've only got a small saucepan, a small colander'll suffice," he responded. "Them ones over 'ere are only sixpence."

Churchill felt a jolt of worry as she noticed Mrs Spooner beginning to move away from them.

"Well, that gives us something to think about, doesn't it, Miss Pemberley? Thank you for your help, kind sir. We'd better be on our way now."

The two ladies began to sidle away after Mrs Spooner.

"I knew the pair o' you weren't goin' to buy nothin' from me!" the market trader shouted after them. "Time-wasters!"

Mrs Spooner had stopped at a crockery stall nearby.

Churchill gave Pemberley a gentle prod with her elbow. "She's looking at milk jugs now, Pembers. Go over there and pretend you're on the lookout for a new milk jug."

"Why must I be on the lookout for a new milk jug? I'm

quite happy with my milk jug, Mrs Churchill. Why can't you be after a new milk jug?"

Churchill sighed. "Fine. I shall be the one looking for a milk jug."

The two ladies joined Mrs Spooner at the crockery stall and pretended to admire the array of milk jugs, teapots and sugar bowls laid out before them.

"I do like a white milk jug with blue stripes," declared Mrs Churchill. "Is that the sort of milk jug you like, Miss Pemberley?"

"I do, though the one I have at the moment has a cow's face on it. I particularly like milk jugs with animals on them."

"I can't see any with animals on here, but there are a few stripy ones that tickle my fancy." Churchill turned casually to Mrs Spooner. "Is there a particular type of milk jug you favour?"

"Not really," the lady replied morosely. She had downturned eyes and a drawn face. "As long as they don't dribble, I don't mind too much what they look like."

"There's nothing worse than a milk jug that dribbles," agreed Churchill. "I abhor such things."

"I wouldn't go quite so far as to say that," replied Mrs Spooner, "but they can certainly be a nuisance. I don't like dribbling milk all over the tablecloth."

"Absolutely not, because then it requires washing, doesn't it? And a rather swift laundering at that, because if it's left too long it's liable to smell." Churchill adopted a more sympathetic expression and lowered her voice. "I hope you don't mind me inquiring, but are you Mrs Spooner? I couldn't help but notice the fact that you're in mourning clothes. And of course the whole village has been extremely shaken by the sad demise of poor Mr Spooner."

Mrs Spooner gave a sad nod. "Yes, it's been an awful few days."

"Have the police made any progress with their investigation?"

"Not that I know of."

"That's Inspector Mappin for you, I'm afraid. He can be a little slow about these things. You wouldn't happen to have heard of Churchill's Detective Agency, would you? I'm Mrs Churchill and this is my trusty assistant, Miss Pemberley. And somewhere around here is our four-legged assistant, Oswald. Between us we've solved a number of important cases."

"I think I shall leave it up to the police, Mrs Churchill. I don't really want to start employing a private detective."

"Oh, goodness," replied Churchill, "I certainly didn't intend to create the impression that I was soliciting my services, Mrs Spooner. I should never like to charge a lady in mourning for any work undertaken to discover who had murdered her husband. I only meant to say that Miss Pemberley and I have solved a number of cases in the past, so we may be able to offer some assistance. We require absolutely nothing from you at all, but if you do want our help…"

"Is there some sort of catch?"

"No! Absolutely no catch. All we're doing is assisting with the investigation to find the person who did this dreadful thing to your husband."

"I see. Well, I was rather hoping Inspector Mappin would be able to sort it out."

"I'm sure he's capable of it, but he has been known to take his time over these things."

"Has he really? But he's a police inspector."

"Yes, he is. But between you and me, Mrs Spooner, he's not a particularly efficient one. Miss Pemberley and I, on the other hand, are a super-sleuthing duo. I'm quite sure we'll find out who murdered your husband before Inspector Mappin does."

"Really?"

"We shall certainly do our best, Mrs Spooner, at no cost or outlay to yourself. If you're able to tell us a bit about your husband, that's really all we need for the time being."

Mrs Spooner shuffled from one foot to the other and pursed her lips in thought. "All right, then." She glanced around her. "But perhaps we'd better discuss it somewhere more private. You never know who's listening in a place like this. Maybe we could take a little stroll by the river."

Chapter 10

Ducks quacked, the sun shone and Oswald sniffed among the rushes as the three ladies followed the path that ran alongside the river.

"What sort of chap was your husband, Mrs Spooner?" asked Churchill.

"He was a thoroughly decent man. We were married for twenty-seven years and I loved every moment of it." Her voice cracked and she dabbed at her nose with her handkerchief.

"You loved every moment? That's very impressive indeed. Do you mind me asking when you last saw him?"

"It was just before he went to ring the bells that morning."

"What was his mood like at that point?"

"He was his usual self, really. Excited about ringing the bells."

"He enjoyed ringing them regularly, is that right?"

"Oh, yes. He loved it. He always enjoyed making a noise."

"Yes, we've heard that."

"You've probably heard that some of the villagers were quite annoyed about it. Some people are dreadfully grumpy about such things."

"They certainly are. There was definitely nothing troubling him before he went to ring the bells, would you say?"

"No, I don't think so."

"Had there been a falling out with anybody that you knew of?"

"Well, all the other bell-ringers had left and joined the team at South Bungerly."

"Do you know why?"

"They're all uneducated, lunk-headed oafs who have no idea what the end of a bell rope is for, let alone have the capacity to ring a bell in time." She paused to blow her nose. "That's what Jeremy said, anyway."

"I see. We're trying to establish who may have wished him real harm."

"One of them, no doubt. Probably Mr Whiplark. He was the one who maintained the bells. And vandalised them, too, I don't doubt."

"There certainly appears to have been motive."

"Indeed! I can't understand why Inspector Mappin doesn't just go and arrest the lot of them!"

"What about Mr Purseglove?"

"He's not a bell-ringer."

"I realise that, but he did have a bit of a to-do with your husband."

"Yes, he did. That's because he's a pig-faced scoundrel with a void between his ears so large you could park a motorcar sideways in it."

"Is that so?"

"That's what Jeremy said about him. I don't know him all that well, but I've always found his wife to be perfectly pleasant."

"It seems as though your husband fell out with a lot of people."

"Not at all. *They* fell out with *him*."

"I see. Is there anyone else who fell out with him?"

"No, but there was a very upsetting incident just a week before his death."

"Was there really? Do tell."

"First of all, I must regale you with an old family tale."

"Golly! Let's hear it, then, Mrs Spooner." Although her interest was piqued, Churchill hoped the story wouldn't go on too long, as she could already feel a little rumble in her tummy.

"Jeremy's father owned Lidcup Jam Factory," began Mrs Spooner. "At least, that's what they call it these days; it used to be Spooner's Jam Factory. Jeremy's father was descended from a long line of jam-makers."

"How interesting."

"Jeremy had an older sister, Jemima, and the pair started work at the factory as soon as they were knee-high to a grasshopper. Jemima was very good at her work, whereas Jeremy was considered to be rather lazy. Quite unfairly I must add! So Jemima was the favourite, and the factory passed to her rather than Jeremy when old Mr Spooner died."

"Oh dear."

"It was very short-sighted of old Mr Spooner, because what happens when a daughter is the heir? She marries and all her property is passed to her husband. That's exactly what happened when Jemima married Sidney Lidcup. Jeremy was convinced that Sidney had married for jam rather than for love."

"Mr Lidcup only wanted the factory, you mean?"

"Exactly. He swept Jemima off her feet and showered her with gifts and affection. That all came to an abrupt end as soon as they were married and he'd got his claws into the factory, just as Jeremy had predicted."

"Do Mr and Mrs Lidcup still own the factory today?"

"Just Sidney now, I'm afraid. Jemima died ten years ago after choking on a fishbone. And now the factory is well and truly out of our family and firmly in Sidney's hands. There is – or should I say *was*? – only one thing Jeremy had that Sidney didn't."

"What was that?"

"The secret family recipe for plum jam. In the heyday of Spooner's Jam Factory, people travelled from all over Dorset to sample it. The recipe was highly prized, and it had been passed down through generation after generation of Jeremy's family. Fortunately, he managed to steal it from the factory after it passed into Jemima's hands."

"Crikey!"

"Jeremy held on to that one special recipe for forty years and refused to allow Sidney anywhere near it. Sidney asked for it many times, but Jeremy took great pleasure in refusing him."

"I bet he did."

"But then a week before Jeremy died, the plum recipe went missing."

"Oh dear. How did that happen?"

"It was usually kept under lock and key, but Jeremy accidentally left it lying on the dining table when he decided to make his latest batch."

"And someone took it?"

"Yes. Our dining room window overlooks a busy lane. Anybody passing by would have been able to peer in and see what was on the dining table right by the window. And as fate would have it, it happened to be quite warm that day, so the window was open. Jeremy loved making jam. That was to be expected, I suppose. It was in his blood."

"Ugh!" responded Pemberley.

"What's the matter?" asked Churchill.

"I can't bear the thought of there being jam in blood."

"It's just a saying, Miss Pemberley. You're interrupting the story. Do go on, Mrs Spooner."

"Jeremy had popped the recipe on the table before going off to Farmer Drumhead's orchard to pick the plums. When he got home, he couldn't find it anywhere. It was gone!"

"Someone passing by in the lane outside must have seen it on the dining table and taken it," mused Churchill.

"Yes! And Jeremy was certain that it was his brother-in-law, Mr Lidcup."

"But how could Mr Lidcup have known that the recipe would be lying around on the dining table?"

"He often walks down our lane. Hyacinth Lane, it's called. He's rather friendly with Miss Harpum who lives a few doors down at Tulip Cottage, you see. Make of that what you will."

"So you're sure that it was Mr Lidcup who stole the recipe but you didn't actually see him do it."

"We didn't see him take it, but it had to have been him. It wouldn't have given him any trouble at all to just slip his arm in through the window and whisk the recipe away. My poor husband was very upset."

"Did he confront Mr Lidcup about it?"

"He planned to go and ask for it back, but he never got the chance."

"Have you related this sorry tale to Inspector Mappin?"

"Oh, yes."

"And is he following it up as a line of investigation?"

"I hope so. Apparently, he and Sidney like to play tennis together, so he's planning on asking him about it the next time they play. I do wish he'd hurry up about it. Sidney Lidcup is nothing but a half-brained, dim-witted rogue with the manners of a flea-bitten goat."

"Gosh. Is that what your husband said about him?"

"No, I just came up with it myself!"

Chapter 11

"THAT WAS AN EXTREMELY informative conversation with Mrs Spooner," said Churchill once she and Pemberley had finished their walk by the river with the grieving widow. "Most importantly, we now have her blessing to investigate her husband's murder."

"Do we have her blessing?"

"She didn't say no, did she?"

"No, but she didn't exactly give us her blessing. Although I suppose she did speak freely to us about her husband and the most likely suspects."

"That'll do for us, Pembers. And there are so many suspects! So many people we need to speak to. What did you make of the curious jam recipe story?"

"It was rather odd wasn't it? I simply cannot understand why Mr Spooner would have left such a prized recipe on a table beside an open window overlooking a lane his brother-in-law regularly walked up and down."

"Rather careless of him, wasn't it? It'll be interesting to see whether or not that recipe turns out to be in the possession of Mr Lidcup. Not that it's terribly relevant to the murder investigation. I can't think what motive Mr Lidcup would have had for murdering his brother-in-law."

"The only possible motive I can think of is that he wanted the recipe."

"Which, according to Mrs Spooner's account, he now has. Where does Mrs Higginbath live?"

"Oh, no. We don't have to visit her, do we?"

"I share your reluctance, Pembers, but she's retained us to find that figurine. I think we need to take note of Mr Sawyer's suggestion and find out if she has a photograph of it. It'll be easier to find if there is one."

Pemberley sighed. "Oh, all right. She's on Netherwort Lane."

"Which is where?"

"It's the road that runs behind the library."

A short while later, the two ladies and their dog came to a stop outside Mrs Higginbath's terraced house. Churchill glanced up and down the road, surveying the little gold-brick houses and their pretty front gardens.

"I see the postbox." She pointed a finger at it. "That's the one Mrs Higginbath must have nipped to when she was out posting her letter. About fifty yards away, would you say?"

"Yes, I think so."

"How long do you think it would take to walk there? No more than a minute, I'd wager. Much less than a minute, in fact. I would say half a minute when you consider the brisk pace Mrs Higginbath walks at. All in all, she was probably only away from her house for a minute or two. The figurine thief must have been walking along this path when he spotted her door lying open. Very opportune indeed."

Mrs Higginbath's door suddenly swung open and the librarian glared out at them.

"Oh, hello," said Churchill. "We haven't even knocked yet."

"I heard voices," responded Mrs Higginbath. "Have you found it?"

"No, not yet. We're still making inquiries, Mrs Higginbath. We were wondering if you had a photograph of the missing figurine."

"Why would I have a photograph of it?"

"It's always advisable to take photographs of valuable items, Mrs Higginbath, in case they're stolen. A photograph comes in useful when trying to find them again."

"Oh, I see. I didn't think of that."

"I hadn't either, but having only recently heard the tip, I shall be taking photographs of all my valuable items from now on. I have some rather nice plates that I brought down with me from London."

"Good. So what do we do if I don't have a photograph? Does that mean it'll never be found?"

"Perhaps a sketch would do," suggested Pemberley.

"A sketch?" responded Mrs Higginbath. "I can't sketch!"

"I'm not so terribly bad at sketching," said Pemberley.

"My trusty assistant's right," said Churchill. "She really is rather good at sketching."

"How about you describe the ornament to me in great detail, Mrs Higginbath, and I'll try to draw it?" suggested Pemberley.

Mrs Higginbath gave an acquiescent grunt. "All right, then, but it sounds like it's going to be rather a long-winded process. And if you don't manage to find the ornament after all this..."

"I'm sure this will really boost our chances of finding it," said Churchill.

"Good grief! That's not the sort of thing you usually draw, Miss Pemberley," said Mrs Thonnings when she visited the two ladies in their office that afternoon. She turned her head one way and then the other as she examined the picture of the courting couple on Pemberley's desk. "It almost makes me blush. Who are they?"

"Nobody," replied Pemberley, looking up from her copy of *The Havana Heist*.

"But they must both be somebody! They look very much in love." She placed a hand on her bosom. "It makes me think back to my first marriage."

"They're not real people," replied Pemberley. "They're two characters from an ornament Mrs Higginbath had stolen."

"Mrs Higginbath stole it?"

"No, someone stole it from Mrs Higginbath."

"Someone stole from Mrs Higginbath? Must have been a brave person. What was Mrs Higginbath doing with an ornament like that? I've never really thought of her as the romantic type."

"No one thought of her as the romantic type," responded Churchill, "until now. Anyway, what brings you here today, Mrs Thonnings? We're very busy."

"Right. Well, I'll make it quick." She sat down at Churchill's desk and smoothed her red hair. "Are you investigating the murder of Mr Spooner, by any chance?"

"Yes. We have his widow's official blessing to do so."

"Do you indeed? That is a relief. I'm sure you'll soon have it all solved, in that case. Have you spoken to Mrs Harris recently?"

"No."

"You need to, because she saw a flickering light in the bell tower."

"Did she indeed? Recently?"

"Yes, recently! She saw it the night before Mr Spooner was murdered. It's widely believed that the murderer must have snuck in there overnight, isn't it? Well, Mrs Harris lives on Horn Hill, which offers a commanding view over the village. She said she happened to look out of her window that night and notice a light in the bell tower. Apparently, it was flickering and wobbling about, as if it were a torch being held by someone climbing the steps. At the time she assumed the sexton was up to something. He's a bit of a funny one, isn't he? But now she's reflected on it, she's certain she must have unwittingly seen the murderer! He would have struggled to get up the steps in the dark, so he would have needed a light to see where he was going and loosen the bolts on the bell. That great, heavy bell. Oh, poor Mr Spooner!"

"That's exceptionally interesting, Mrs Thonnings. Did Mrs Harris say what time it was when she saw the light?"

"A little after three o'clock. She hadn't been able to sleep because Mr Harris was snoring, so she sat beside the window for a bit."

"What a stroke of luck that Mr Harris was snoring! Otherwise we wouldn't have been able to identify the time the killer was going about his business in the bell tower. Has she told Inspector Mappin about this?"

"Oh, yes. He's taken a full statement from her."

"That's a shame. I always prefer it when we manage to gather more information than him. Never mind. This is useful information, Mrs Thonnings. Very useful indeed."

Chapter 12

"BEFORE WE GET STARTED, I'd like to thank Mr Barnfather and his good lady wife for 'ostin' us this evenin'," said Mr Whiplark. "And I'm sure you'll all join me in welcomin' Miss Churchley and Mrs Pember'ill to our little meetin'."

"*Mrs Churchill* and *Miss Pemberley*," corrected Churchill.

"And Oswald," added Pemberley.

"We're very honoured to 'ave yer joinin' us this evenin', ladies," continued Mr Whiplark. "I even brushed me beard fer this 'ere meetin'."

"And very nice it looks, too, Brian," said Mrs Barnfather as she poured out numerous cups of tea. She was a slender lady with neatly waved grey hair.

Mr Barnfather sat upright in his armchair. He had donned a jacket and tie to mark the occasion.

Churchill and Pemberley were seated on the settee, while the bell-ringers occupied a set of dining chairs that had presumably been brought into the Barnfathers' parlour from the dining room. Mr Whiplark was squatting on a leather-covered footstool, his knees almost as high as his shoulders.

"Who's chairing?" asked Mr Barnfather in a stiff voice. "Shall I do it or would you like to, Brian?"

"I'll do it," replied Mr Whiplark.

"And whose turn is it to take the minutes?" asked Mr Barnfather, turning to the bell-ringers on the dining chairs.

"I'm sure there's no need for minutes to be taken," said Churchill. "My assistant and I only intended for this to be an informal chat."

Mr Barnfather gave her a stern glance. "Everything must be written down, Mrs Churchill. We have rules."

"I see."

"I'll take the minutes," said a young man with oiled hair. He wore a stiff collar and a brown pullover.

"Thank you, Anthony," said Mr Barnfather. He turned to Churchill. "This is Anthony Thurkell. He rings the number two bell."

"Or used ter," said Mr Whiplark.

"Used to," agreed Mr Thurkell with a nod. "I can't get on the bells so easily now we're at St Baldred's."

"Give it time, Anthony," responded Mr Barnfather. "We're a superior team to the ringers at St Baldred's. It won't be long before you've a firm grip on the number two bell rope there."

"My assistant and I would like to know what the disagreement between yourselves and the late Mr Jeremy Spooner was about," said Churchill, keen to get the discussion underway. "I should add that we have the blessing of his widow to investigate his untimely death."

"All in good time, Mrs Churchill," responded Mr Barnfather, "but before we discuss that, can I confirm that everyone was happy with the minutes from the last meeting?"

"I'm chairin'," said Mr Whiplark. "And this is an extra-special meetin'. We don't need to be discussin' minutes from the last meetin'. We need to be tellin' these good ladies 'ere all about Jeremy and who's done 'im in."

"We're not following the usual agenda?" asked Mr Barnfather.

"No, we ain't. Not this evenin'."

Having completed the pouring out of the tea, Mrs Barnfather carried a tray around for everyone to take a cup. "Are you sure you're all right down there, Brian?" she asked. "That pouffe is no place for the chair of the meeting. You should take my husband's seat."

"I'm not swapping," said Mr Barnfather. "Not with my back."

"I've told yer before and I'll tell yer again, Doreen, I'm perfeckly 'appy on the pouffe," said Mr Whiplark, taking a cup from the tray. "Now then, Miss Churchley. Shall we answer them questions o' yours?"

"Yes," she replied, keen not to waste any more time correcting him. "Why did you all leave the bell-ringing team at St Swithun's?"

"My hands couldn't take it anymore," said a wiry man with wispy white hair and eyebrows. He held out his palms. "Look at the calluses."

Churchill gave his hands a cursory glance.

"He had us ringing quarter peals every evening," the wiry man added.

"Quarter peals?"

"Twelve hundred and fifty changes," explained Mr Barnfather. "It typically takes about forty-five minutes. Quarter peals are usually only rung for special events, but Spooner had us practising them every night."

"It was more than an old man's hands could take," said the wiry man. "Sometimes big bits of skin would come off!"

Churchill felt Pemberley shudder next to her. "How unpleasant," she said. "May I make a note of your name?"

"Mr Cogg."

"Malcolm Cogg, number four bell," clarified Mr Barnfather.

"And if I ever hear 'Double Norwich' again, I'll lose my mind," a red-haired man in a grubby shirt piped up.

"Hear what?"

"'Double Norwich Court Bob Major'," replied the red-haired man. "A ringing method. Spooner was obsessed with it. We got so fed up that we reached the point where even a simple plain hunt would have been preferable."

The other bell-ringers nodded in agreement.

"May I make a note of your name as well?" asked Churchill.

"Mr Linney. Alfred Linney. Number six bell. Hopefully one day I'll get to number eight bell!"

"I'm number seven bell," added Mr Barnfather. "And Spooner was always number eight."

"He always got the biggest bell," said Mr Cogg with a sigh. "None of us ever stood a chance of ringing that huge tenor. Poor Saul here's been on the treble number one bell for fifteen years."

A wide man whose arms were folded over his chest gave a nod. "Nearly sixteen, to be precise. I'm Saul Melding, for your notebook, Mrs Churchill."

"Thank you, Mr Melding." Churchill wrote this down. "Just for completeness, who's on the number five bell?"

"Me," said Mr Whiplark, raising his hand.

Churchill turned to a curly-haired man with thick, greying whiskers. "Then you must be on the number three."

"Aye," he replied.

"Mr Veltom," explained Mr Barnfather. "Miles Veltom."

"Thank you," said Churchill. "Well, it seems to me that each and every one of you had a grievance against Mr Spooner."

Wiry Mr Cogg nodded. "There was hell to pay if you didn't grip the sally properly, or if you accidentally let go of your tail end."

"He had high standards," agreed Mr Thurkell, "and he was very unforgiving. He suspended me for three weeks last Christmas after I accidentally broke a stay. I got a little carried away after all the mulled wine. We had to drink plenty of it to get through full peals."

"Full peals?"

"Three hours," clarified Mr Barnfather. "Five thousand changes."

"So I had some mulled wine," continued the young man, "and pulled a little too hard. The stay broke and the bell went right over, pulling up the rope – and me with it!"

"There he was, danglin' from the ceiling o' the ringin' chamber!" said Mr Whiplark with a cackle. "We all 'ad a bit of a laugh, as you do. And as steeple keeper, I know it ain't too difficult to replace a stay. But Spooner weren't 'avin' none of it."

"He wasn't the least bit amused," added Mr Barnfather.

"He accused me of abusing the position of belfry man," said Mr Thurkell. "Three weeks' suspension! It felt much longer."

"Would it be safe to say that you'd all had enough, so you collectively decided to resign as bell-ringers the week before Mr Spooner's death?" asked Churchill.

"That's correct," replied Mr Barnfather. "We held a meeting, and a vote of no confidence in Mr Spooner was passed. But the stubborn fellow chose to ignore it! After that, we all left and went over to St Baldred's."

"And we know 'ow it looks," added Mr Whiplark. "We all got fed up with 'im, and then 'e went and got 'imself murdered. So it must've been one of us what done it! But it weren't me… Even though I were the one what looked after them bells."

"It wasn't me either," said Mr Linney.

The other bell-ringers also muttered their denials.

"I haven't been up in the belfry for ten years," added Mr Cogg.

"I went up there a few weeks ago to fit the muffles," said Mr Linney, "but that was all."

"Can your wives vouch for the fact that you were all at home the night before Mr Spooner's death?" asked Churchill. "From eight o'clock until the following morning?"

Most of the bell-ringers nodded.

"I don't have a wife," said Mr Thurkell.

"I 'aven't got one, neither!" protested Mr Whiplark.

"I do," said Mr Barnfather. "Doreen!" he called over his shoulder.

"Yes, love?" Mrs Barnfather stepped into the room, wiping her hands on her apron.

"The night before Spooner died," began Mr Barnfather. "I was here the entire time, wasn't I?"

"Yes, that's right."

"From eight o'clock in the evening until the morning. That's right, isn't it?"

"Yes, dear. You were home all the time."

"Very good." He gave Churchill a smug nod. "There's my alibi for you, Mrs Churchill. If there's anything else you'd like to know, just ask."

"Thank you, Mr Barnfather."

"What abou' me?" protested Mr Whiplark. "I 'aven't got no alibi!"

"I imagine the local constabulary will soon be rounding you up, Brian," replied Mr Barnfather, steepling his fingers.

"But that ain't fair! Just 'cause I was the steeple keeper, an' all! I already know what everyone's thinkin', but it weren't me!"

Mr Cogg leaned forward in his chair. "Mrs Churchill, I'd just like to say right now that I don't believe it was one of us."

"Is that right?"

"Absolutely, and I'll tell you why. We didn't like Jeremy Spooner, and I'm sure that each and every one of us harboured a desire for revenge. But no bell-ringer would have committed murder in such a way. It just isn't possible. The simple reason being that church bells are sacrosanct to us. Not one of us would ever have caused damage to one of our beloved bells. What the murderer did was utter sacrilege."

Chapter 13

"YOU LOOK RATHER tired this morning, Pembers," said Churchill when she arrived at the office to find her assistant already at her desk. "Did the bell-ringers wear you out yesterday evening?"

"No. I stayed up late working on the prayer cushion."

"I'm sure there's really no need for you to do that."

"I'm having trouble fitting everything in, Mrs Churchill. I also want to finish reading *The Havana Heist*, so when I got home last night after the bell-ringer meeting I decided to alternate between a quarter of an hour sewing and a quarter of an hour reading. Before I knew it, it was midnight."

"Goodness!"

"I'm not very good at going to bed late these days."

"I know what you mean. I often find that I'm getting the yawns by eight o'clock. It sounds to me as though you need to make a choice between the sewing and the reading, Pembers. Switching back and forth between the two must be exhausting."

"Oh, it is. I don't know whether I'm coming or going today."

"It's just as well we don't have an important murder case to solve. Oh, hold on, we do. How about I make us some tea? After that and a few iced fancies, I predict you'll feel fully restored."

"I hope so."

"And then we need to go and speak to the Purseglovess."

"What about?"

"If Mrs Purseglove can vouch for the fact that Mr Purseglove was sound asleep at three o'clock on the morning of Mr Spooner's death, we can rule him out as a suspect."

"You're quite certain that the flickering light Mrs Harris saw in the bell tower was the murderer, are you?"

"Very certain indeed. Establishing alibis will be a good way to narrow down our list of suspects. Only two or three of the bell-ringers have no alibi for that time, for example."

"But what if Mrs Barnfather was lying?"

"She doesn't seem like the sort to lie."

"But she may have done. Mr Barnfather strikes me as the sort of person you might feel pressured to agree with. He made her provide an alibi in front of everyone, and she may have felt too embarrassed to refuse. Don't you think?"

"I suppose so, now you come to mention it."

"It would have caused an awkward silence If she'd refused, and then an uncomfortable atmosphere."

"Yes, it would. I imagine she probably wanted to avoid such a scenario."

"It seems Mr Barnfather was rather clever in forcing his wife to provide an alibi for him there and then. He put her on the spot; she couldn't possibly have said anything different."

Churchill made a note of this in her notebook. "Having crossed him off my list, I suppose I'd better put him down as a 'maybe' again. Isn't it a shame that people aren't always as honest as one would like them to be, Pembers?"

"Perhaps Mrs Barnfather was telling the truth, but for the moment we can't be sure."

"Indeed. In that case, even if Mrs Purseglove provides an alibi for her husband we must treat it with a pinch of salt."

"Yes, I think so. It would be a different matter if she were speaking to the police, I'd say, because lying to the police is a very serious matter."

"Inspector Mappin is certainly backed up by the strong arm of the law, there's no doubt about that. But let's speak to the Pursegloves anyway. Even if they lie to us, I can usually rely on my gut instinct and women's intuition to detect the truth."

"That's the important thing, Mrs Churchill. Didn't you say you were about to put the kettle on?"

"Yes. Thank you for the reminder, Pembers."

"What can I do for you this time?" asked Mr Purseglove when he answered his front door.

Churchill didn't like the way his small, beady eyes bored into her. "We have another question for you about Mr Spooner. And we'd also like to speak to your wife, if possible."

"I suppose you'd better come in."

"Good morning, ladies!" beamed Mrs Purseglove as they entered the front room. She was wearing a floral housecoat and held a feather duster in her hand. "You've caught me at it, I'm afraid. Tidying up Terence's books and newspapers!"

The clutter Churchill recalled from her last visit appeared to have been picked up and redistributed around the room.

"Would you like some tea and cake?" Mrs Purseglove asked.

"You're a lady after our own hearts, Mrs Purseglove."

Mr Purseglove sank into an armchair and folded his arms across his scruffy cardigan. "Managed to narrow down the list of suspects yet, Mrs Churchill?" he asked.

"Not yet."

"Thought as much. I wasn't the only one who was tempted to wrap a bell rope around Spooner's neck."

"Have you any suggestions as to who else we should be speaking to?"

"Most of the village, I'd say."

"That's very helpful. Thank you."

Mrs Purseglove came in with the tea tray. "I made some lovely lemon and raisin cake this morning," she said. "You must try it."

"Raisin?" queried Churchill weakly, still mindful of Mrs Higginbath's legless spider description.

"And lemon! You must have a slice."

"She'll be ever so offended if you don't," added Mr Purseglove.

"It sounds as though I couldn't possibly say no!" Churchill forced a smile.

"These two ladies are looking for Mr Spooner's killer," Mr Purseglove explained to his wife.

"Indeed we are," responded Churchill. "With the official blessing of his poor widow."

"Oh, that's nice," said Mrs Purseglove, handing

Churchill a slice of cake. "How lovely to have her blessing."

"You'd think the police would have solved the case by now," her husband commented. "That's their job, isn't it?"

"Yes, but isn't it lovely that these two ladies are taking it upon themselves to have a go?" said Mrs Purseglove. "Women are so much more observant than men, wouldn't you say, Mrs Churchill?"

"We do tend to possess excellent powers of observation, yes."

"I can certainly agree with that," said Mr Purseglove through a mouthful of cake. "Nothing gets past my missis."

"We would like to ask you, Mr Purseglove, where you were the night before Mr Spooner was murdered," asked Churchill.

"All right, then."

"Where were you?"

"Here, of course. And if it was night-time I'd have been in bed."

"Can you vouch for that, Mrs Purseglove?"

"Oh, yes. He never goes anywhere."

"I do!" protested her husband.

"Where?"

"The Wagon and Carrot."

"Apart from the pub."

Mr Purseglove chewed another mouthful of cake as he considered this. "I went over to Downton Buckheath the other week."

"To pick up the coal?"

"Yes. To pick up the coal."

Mrs Purseglove gave Churchill and Pemberley a broad smile. "My husband couldn't possibly be a murderer, you see. He hardly ever leaves the house!"

"But you do go to the church, don't you, Mr Purseglove?" asked Churchill.

"Yes, but that's only over the road. It doesn't count."

"Did you visit the church the night before Mr Spooner was murdered?"

"What are you implying? Are you asking if it was me who loosened the bolts on the tenor bell?"

"He wouldn't know how to loosen a bolt if you gave him a spanner and an instruction book," said Mrs Purseglove.

"I do know how to loosen bolts!" he snapped.

"Are you sure you want to go admitting that in front of these two lady detectives?"

"Yes, because I have nothing to hide! I know how to loosen bolts and I also threatened to wrap a bell rope around Mr Spooner's neck. I don't mind admitting it at all. But does that make me a murderer? No!"

"My husband isn't a murderer, Mrs Churchill. He may be many things, but he's not a murderer. Is something the matter with your cake? You haven't touched it."

"I've just been a little distracted by our conversation, Mrs Purseglove. I shall get round to it in a moment."

"Of course. How's the rest of your investigation going?"

"It's going very well indeed, thank you. It seems a lot of people didn't like Mr Spooner, including the whole gang of bell-ringers."

"I hear they've all gone off to St Baldred's," said Mr Purseglove. "I hope they stay there. I don't want any of their racket back here in Compton Poppleford."

"Mr Spooner was certainly an interesting character," mused his wife. "And not very well-liked. My cousin had a few dealings with him before his death."

"Is that so?"

"Yes, he's a reporter for the *Compton Poppleford Gazette*. Apparently, Mr Spooner had a story for him, but he died before Smithy could get to the bottom of it."

Churchill knew immediately who Mrs Purseglove was referring to, she'd met him a number of times in the past. "Is your cousin Smithy Miggins, by any chance?"

"Yes! Do you know him?"

"We certainly do! And on the basis of what you've just told us, Mrs Purseglove, I think we may need to have a little chat with him."

Chapter 14

A SHORT WHILE LATER, Churchill and Pemberley arrived at the red-brick offices of the *Compton Poppleford Gazette*. A tall woman with dyed black hair and painted eyebrows answered the door.

Churchill introduced herself, then added, "Please may we speak with your reporter, Smithy Miggins?"

"He's out on a story."

"Any idea when he'll be back?"

"No."

"Thank you. You've been enormously helpful."

"Rude woman," muttered Churchill as the two ladies walked away. "Why are people so rude these days? I'm sure there must have been a time when everyone was helpful to their fellow man."

"And woman."

"Of course."

"And dog," added Pemberley, looking down proudly at Oswald, who was walking along beside them.

"Indeed. Now, let's go back to the office and fetch your sketch of Mrs Higginbath's figurine. Then we can repair to the Wagon and Carrot when it opens. Do you remember Mr Sawyer saying that fancy ornaments tended to sell quite well in there? We need to find out if anyone's seen it."

"Ho, ho," chuckled the bartender at the Wagon and Carrot, which was surprisingly busy considering it was only lunchtime. "A naughty picture, eh?"

"No, it's not a naughty picture," retorted Churchill. "It's a sketch of a courting couple."

"Exactly! Ho, ho."

"It's an ornament!" she snapped. "A valuable eighteenth-century porcelain figurine, to be precise."

"Oh, is it now?" He picked up a tankard and began wiping it with a grubby cloth.

"I was wondering whether you might have seen it."

"I'd remember if I'd seen a naughty ornament like that."

"You haven't seen it, then?"

"Why would I 'ave seen it?"

Churchill leaned in. "I've heard tell that certain items may be bought and sold in such a place as this."

The bartender stopped wiping the tankard and gave her a fierce scowl. "I'd like ter know where you've 'eard such nonsense!"

"I'm not holding you responsible at all; nor am I casting aspersions on the integrity of this fine establishment. I'm merely on the trail of a stolen ornament—"

"*Stolen?* What sort of public 'ouse d'yer think this is? The Pig and Scythe?"

"I do apologise if I've caused offence. I..."

"If you wanna find the sort what steals naughty ornaments, the Pig and Scythe's yer best bet. We don't get none o' them types in 'ere."

Churchill reflected, all too late, that she had made a mistake in approaching the bartender. She decided to appease him by ordering a couple of brandy and vermouths. Then the two ladies surveyed the pub regulars around the room.

"Who do we ask about the naughty ornament, Pembers? I fear we may get ourselves into a spot of trouble if we even suggest that any wrongdoing occurs on these premises."

"I don't know, Mrs Churchill, but I do know that Smithy Miggins is standing just over there."

"Out on a story! Well spotted, Pembers."

The lank-haired news reporter stood laughing and joking with a group of loud men; a social situation Churchill found vaguely intimidating.

"What you need to do, Pembers, is lure him over."

Pemberley choked on her drink. "Lure him over? How am I supposed to lure him over?"

"I don't know. You're a seasoned private detective. Surely you have some skills in luring?"

"I'm your secretary, Mrs Churchill. You're the one who should be doing all the luring."

"Oh, I would, but I'm just no good at it. There's something about you, Pembers, that suggests you'd be far better at it than me."

"I wouldn't even know where to start! You're making me all shy and bashful, Mrs Churchill, and I shall feel like going home if you put any more pressure on me to lure Smithy Miggins over."

"Okay, let's forget about the luring. What shall we do to fetch him here? I don't want to walk over there and interrupt them. They'll all turn and scowl at me and make me feel uncomfortable."

"Maybe we could use Oswald."

Churchill looked down at the little dog standing by their feet. "Now there's an idea. He's looking particularly well-behaved at the moment, isn't he? People often respond favourably to Oswald. What can we have him do?"

"I could find something to surreptitiously toss at Smithy Miggins's feet, then Oswald could be instructed to go over and fetch it. That would precipitate an encounter with him."

"That's an excellent idea, Pembers. What do you propose to toss at Smithy Miggins?"

Pemberley opened her handbag. "I have something in here that might work." She pulled out what appeared to be a small, soft ball. "A few pairs of rolled up stockings," she said. "I call it Oswald's indoor ball. It's the sort of ball you can throw about indoors without damaging anything."

"Perfect! All you need to do now is throw it at Smithy Miggins."

"But I need to do it in such a way that he won't know it was me. I think if you could stand in front and block his view of me, I could sort of roll it around your feet and get Oswald to chase it that way."

"Not a bad idea, Pembers. However, I take offence at the suggestion that I could somehow block his view of you. I'm not *that* wide."

"You're just wide enough, Mrs Churchill. Should we try it?"

"Yes, let's give it a go."

Churchill positioned herself in front of Pemberley so that Smithy Miggins would be unable to see what she was doing. Then Pemberley stooped down and rolled the little stocking ball toward the reporter's feet.

"Fetch the ball, Oswald!" she whispered to her dog. "Go on, fetch it! Go and fetch the ball!"

Oswald remained where he was, his tongue lolling out of his mouth.

"Fetch the ball, Oswald! Look, Mummy's just thrown it for you. It's over there by that man's feet. Go and fetch it!"

The little dog did nothing.

"Why isn't he doing anything, Pembers?"

"He will in a minute. He's thinking about it."

"Does he usually take this long to think about chasing a ball?"

"No. I suspect it's because we're somewhere unfamiliar. I've never thrown a ball for him in a public house before."

"Go on, Oswald!" urged Churchill. "Go and fetch the ball!"

The little dog gave a little woof and sat down.

"Oh dear," said Churchill. "I was so hopeful that your plan would work. Now your stocking ball is over by Smithy Miggins's feet. How are we supposed to fetch it? If the dog isn't going to, you'll have to do it."

"I'm not going into that group of men to fetch my little ball," said Pemberley firmly. "How embarrassing!"

"I would go myself," said Churchill, "only it's not my ball."

"But it was your idea, Mrs Churchill."

"It wasn't my idea to throw a ball at Smithy Miggins. That was your idea, Pembers."

"It was your idea to distract him with something, so that's what I did! And now it's all gone wrong and I'll never see my little stocking ball again." Pemberley's lower lip began to wobble.

"Oh, all right. I didn't realise the ball was so important to you."

"It's not important to me. It's important to Oswald!"

"If it's that important to him, why hasn't he gone to fetch it?"

"Because he's shy!"

"I've never known him be shy before."

"I think it's just a phase he's going through."

"Well, if he's going to be a useful detective dog, we could do without him going through phases, Pembers. We really needed him to be our distraction and introduction to Smithy Miggins. Now I'll have to stride over there, fetch the ball and make a complete fool of myself."

Chapter 15

CHURCHILL LEFT Pemberley's side and reluctantly made her way toward the group of men, most of whom were loudly guffawing. She kept her eye fixed on the little stocking ball nestled beside Smithy Miggins's scruffy boot and mulled over what she was going to say to the reporter. She wondered how to explain what the ball was doing there, and how she could move on from that topic to finding out what Mr Spooner had been talking to him about.

Her steps slowed as she drew closer to the men. She turned back to glance at Pemberley, hoping for a little reassurance. Standing by the bar with her dog, Pemberley gave Churchill an encouraging nod. They exchanged a smile and Churchill continued on her way.

None of the group noticed her as she approached.

"Excuse me," she said, but her words were drowned out by another round of roaring laughter. Feeling impatient, Churchill stooped down to grab the ball. She almost had it within her grasp when she felt a sudden weight on her back.

She heard the word "Oof!" as someone tumbled over her and a tankard went crashing to the floor.

This was swiftly followed by, "*What the…?*"

"What's 'appened?"

Churchill quickly realised she was lying in a puddle of scrumpy. Or at least she hoped it was scrumpy.

"Help!" she called out.

She immediately felt hands beneath her arms, hauling her up onto her feet.

"Are you all right, old lady? Did you have a fall?"

She was helped over to a bench, where a group of concerned faces filled her vision.

"I'm quite all right, thank you, and no I didn't have a fall. I was merely retrieving something I had dropped."

A heavy-jowled man, also soaked in scrumpy, picked up the empty tankard. "I thought it was a dog I'd tripped over!"

"It's Mrs Churchill, isn't it?" asked Smithy Miggins.

"Yes, it is," responded Churchill. "Good afternoon, Mr Miggins. We spoke during my investigation into the Earl of Middlemop's death, did we not?"

"That's right. I remember now."

"I do apologise for causing that little accident. I was just in the process of retrieving a ball for my friend's dog. It had accidentally rolled down by your feet, you see."

"It was by my feet? I didn't even see it."

"How about I buy you a nice tankard of scrumpy as an apology?"

"Why does *he* get a tankard of scrumpy?" asked the man who had tripped over Mrs Churchill. "Why not me? *I'm* the one who lost my scrumpy!"

"Very well, I shall buy one for you, too. I'm so sorry I tripped you."

"And what about me?" asked a man in a shabby suit.

Churchill sighed. "How many companions do you have with you here today, Mr Miggins?"

"It's just the five of us."

"I see. Five tankards of scrumpy, then?"

"That's very generous of you, Mrs Churchill."

"Very well. I shall buy them on one condition, Mr Miggins: that you allow me to have a quiet word with you about something."

"The thing is, a reporter never reveals his sources," said Smithy Miggins once Churchill had ordered the tankards and outlined her investigation for him. He leaned against the bar and exhaled a ring of smoke.

"But we know that you spoke to Mr Spooner shortly before his death."

"Who told you that?"

"We prefer not to reveal our sources either. What did you speak to him about? We understand he had something of a grievance."

"Well, that would be telling."

Churchill noticed that his tankard of scrumpy was being rapidly consumed. She ordered him another.

"Why do you want to know, anyway?" he asked. "The police are investigating all that."

"Hapless Inspector Mappin, you mean?"

"That's a little uncalled for. Mappin's all right."

"I'm sure he's very good company indeed when one is playing tennis with him or sitting next to him at a dinner party. But the fact of the matter is, he's rather hopeless at being a detective."

"Is that why you've taken it upon yourselves to solve Spooner's murder?"

"With Mrs Spooner's blessing."

"How do you know she didn't do it?"

"We don't know that. She may well have done. But at the moment we're just trying to understand what was going on in Mr Spooner's life in the days leading up to his death. There may be a clue we have missed."

"Maybe."

As soon as Smithy Miggins had drained his tankard, Churchill handed him a fresh one.

"So what do you say, Mr Miggins? Do you fancy sharing with us what Mr Spooner told you?"

"The trouble is, Mrs Churchill, I can't tell you what he told me because he swore me to secrecy."

"With all due respect, Mr Miggins, poor Mr Spooner is no longer with us. Revealing his secrets now isn't likely to trouble him all that much."

"A promise is a promise, especially when you're in my line of work. Reporters aren't used to giving away other people's secrets."

"How very honourable of you. But let's consider for a moment that you did choose to give away Mr Spooner's secret. What real harm would it cause?"

Smithy Miggins thought about this for a while as he puffed on his cigarette. Then he took a large swig of scrumpy and puffed again. "I suppose he *is* dead now."

"Yes, he is. Do you think the information he revealed to you could lead us to his murderer?"

Churchill waited patiently while he puffed again and drank a little more scrumpy.

"Having thought about it, I suppose it could point to a suspect."

"Interesting. Have you mentioned this to Inspector Mappin?"

"No, I hadn't even considered it. I don't like to reveal other people's secrets, as you know."

"Whatever Mr Spooner's reasons were for you to keep his secret, the chances are they're no longer applicable, wouldn't you say? And if it helps in finding the person who decided to drop an enormous bell on him, revealing his secret might actually provide some sort of justice for his poor grieving widow."

"Well, if you put it like that, Mrs Churchill."

"Perhaps another tankard of scrumpy might persuade you, Mr Miggins?"

"Another tankard of scrumpy might well have a persuasive effect."

"Excellent." Churchill ordered another tankard and hoped it would be the last she had to ply Mr Miggins with.

"Oswald wants to go home," Pemberley muttered in Churchill's ear. "He's bored."

"He'll just have to be patient a little longer," she whispered in reply. "Miggins is on the verge of spilling the beans. Can't Oswald play with his ball?"

"It's all soggy and smells of scrumpy. He doesn't like it anymore."

"Right, well maybe you can pick him up and tickle him or something. Just do whatever it takes to keep him occupied for a few moments longer." Churchill noticed the news reporter's movements were becoming a little clumsier now that the scrumpy was beginning to take effect. "We're almost there, Pembers."

She turned back to Smithy Miggins. "Surely it wouldn't be too difficult to tell myself and my trusty assistant here whatever it was that Mr Spooner was trying to conceal."

"I suppose not."

"You *suppose* not? I've just bought you three tankards of scrumpy, Mr Miggins! I'm hoping you'll be able to tell us Mr Spooner's secret, which, according to you, may point the finger at his murderer. I'd say that was rather important information, wouldn't you?"

He nodded.

"Is the information Mr Spooner wished to keep secret likely to embarrass him?"

"No, it's not embarrassing. And he's dead, anyway, so it wouldn't matter even if it were."

"You're finally coming round to my way of thinking, Mr Miggins. Now, in the interests of time, perhaps you'd like to reveal this piece of secret information? Given that you're a news reporter, I can only assume that he wished to make it public at some stage. Perhaps he wanted it published in the *Compton Poppleford Gazette*."

"Now you mention it, Mrs Churchill, he did suggest that he might want it published."

"Aha! Now we're getting closer to the truth."

"He wanted to publicly shame someone."

"Interesting."

"I can't say for certain, but if the person he wished to publicly shame had found out about it in advance of my writing the article, the said person might have wanted him silenced."

"This all sounds very promising indeed. There are quite a few people who seem to have wanted Mr Spooner silenced, but I imagine the one he wished to publicly shame would be the most likely, wouldn't you?"

"Yes, indeed." He took another large swig of scrumpy. "The truth is, he'd had a very important jam recipe stolen."

"I know about that."

"Really?"

"Yes, Mrs Spooner told us about it. He left it lying on the dining table and assumed Mr Lidcup had stolen it. That's not his great secret, is it?"

"Well yes it is, really."

"Do you mean to tell me I've been plying you with scrumpy only for you to confirm what I already knew?"

"I never have any objections to being plied with scrumpy, Mrs Churchill."

"I can see that."

"I've done all right out of it, haven't I?"

"You have indeed."

"So there you have it. Only to add that Mr Spooner believed Mr Lidcup had stolen his jam recipe, and he was so incensed that he wanted something written in the paper about it. He didn't want Mr Lidcup publicly named; he just wanted to infer that a local jam factory owner might have stolen it. I encouraged him not to name Mr Lidcup, because that could have caused problems with Mr Lidcup's lawyers, of course. But he wanted to implicate Mr Lidcup in the theft of his jam recipe in a roundabout way."

"Thank you Mr Miggins."

"What are you going to do now? Tell Inspector Mappin?"

"In due course, yes. But in the meantime we'll keep this conversation between us. Are you agreed on that?"

The news reporter nodded. "Oh yes, Mrs Churchill. I'm used to keeping confidences, as you know. Any chance of another tankard?"

Chapter 16

"No prizes for guessing who we need to speak to next, Pembers."

The two ladies and their dog had left the Wagon and Carrot and were making their way up the high street.

"That's a shame. I like prizes."

"So do I, but there's a time and a place for them. Mr Lidcup is our man and ideally I'd like to pay him a visit this very afternoon. But I need to go home and wash the scrumpy out of my clothes. I dread to think what the effects of strong cider on Harris tweed might be. While I'm seeing to that, perhaps you could telephone Mr Lidcup and arrange an appointment with him for tomorrow."

"What reason should I give?"

"Tell him we'd like to speak to him about his deceased brother-in-law."

"And if he refuses?"

"I'm sure you'll be able to persuade him."

"But I'm no good at persuading people, Mrs Churchill."

"You're far better at it than you realise, Pembers. If you think it's going to be tricky, tell him we want to have a look around his factory. Factory owners love showing people around their factories."

"How do you know that?"

"Never mind how; it's just a simple fact. Oh, look! Is that Mr Whiplark heading toward us?"

A lean man with a long grey beard was on the approach. "Miss Churchley!" he called out. "Mrs Pember'ill! Just the two ladies I've been lookin' for."

"*Mrs Churchill* and *Miss Pemberley*."

"Yep." He sniffed the air and looked Churchill up and down. "Looks like you've been at the scrumpy, Miss Churchley. Or even *in* the scrumpy by the sight o' you!" He cackled. "What's 'appened?"

"A minor incident at the Wagon and Carrot."

"That's the Wagon and Carrot for yer!" He laughed again. "Now, I've come to tell yer I've got meself an alibi."

"Oh, have you? That's jolly nice to hear."

"She won't tell you nothin', but she's a good enough alibi."

"Wonderful. She can vouch for the fact that you were at home for the entire night before Mr Spooner's death, can she?"

"Oh, yeah. In me caravan, I was. Right where it's parked up now. "You seen me there yerself, didn't yer?"

"We did indeed. Why won't your alibi be able to tell us anything?"

"It's just 'er nature. She don't speak."

"Intriguing."

"Farmer Drum'ead'll back me up."

"Good. And your alibi is a lady friend of yours, is she?"

"Not a friend, as such. She's me 'orse."

"Your horse is your alibi?"

"Yeah, Bessie. I know 'ow it sounds, Miss Churchley, but lemme explain. Bessie don't like night-time. She don't like the dark, see. If I don't check on 'er every few hours she starts whinnyin'."

"Poor Bessie," said Pemberley.

"She's fine as long as I keeps checkin' on 'er, Mrs Pember'ill. And that's where Farmer Drum'ead comes into it. If she starts whinnyin', it's so loud 'e can 'ear 'er all the way over in the farm'ouse. Now, if you ask 'im about that night, 'e'll tell you 'e heard no whinnyin' from Bessie that night. That's because I was checkin' on 'er reg'lar, see, like I always does. If I'd walked down the church, climbed up that bell tower, loosened the bolts on the old bell, climbed back down the bell tower an' walked all the way 'ome again I reckon I'd 'ave been gone at least two hours. Proberly three. Bessie wouldn't 'ave liked that. She'd 'ave been whinnyin'."

"I see," responded Churchill, unsure what to make of the tale. She was feeling the chill from her damp clothes and the scrumpy stench was beginning to turn her stomach.

"So am I in the clear?" he asked hopefully.

"I don't know if I can say that, exactly. A horse is rather an unusual—"

"I know that, Miss Churchley, but it all makes sense, don't it? It's important to me, see. Everyone's pointin' the finger at the man what looked after the bells. An' that's me!"

"Yes. Well, I suppose your alibi will do for now."

"Really?" His face lit up. "Oh, thank you, Miss Churchley!"

"Unless any new evidence comes to light."

"New evidence? What new evidence?"

"I don't know yet. I'm sure you're completely blameless and there's nothing for you to worry about, Mr Whiplark."

"I am!"

"Now, do excuse me. I need to go and get washed up."

Chapter 17

"Welcome to my jam factory, ladies!" enthused Mr Lidcup.

He was a tall, broad man with wavy, oiled hair that looked suspiciously dark for a man of his age. Churchill judged him to be no younger than sixty.

"Is that a dog?" he asked, peering past Pemberley.

"Yes. He's the third member of our team."

"Would he mind waiting outside for the duration of your visit? I don't allow animals inside the factory as a rule. We don't want any dog hairs in the jam!"

"I quite like them," responded Pemberley, "I find they add a bit of flavour."

"Put Oswald outside, Miss Pemberley," instructed Churchill.

"He'll be quite safe out there in the factory yard," said Mr Lidcup. "He won't be able to get beyond the gates. There may even be a few pigeons for him to chase out there!"

"It's a sizeable place you have here, Mr Lidcup," commented Churchill as she glanced around her.

The sweet smell of boiled fruit filled the cavernous building and clouds of steam rose up into its high ceiling. Chopping and whirring sounds came from rows of machines manned by women in white caps and aprons. From the far end of the building came the clank of glass jars as they were gathered and filled with fruity preserves.

Although she had been underwhelmed by her most recent taste of Lidcup's jam, Churchill's mouth began to water.

"It's a big old place, all right," said Mr Lidcup. "Keeps me out of trouble, that's for sure!" He winked, then snapped his fingers at a lady nearby. "Mavis! Caps and aprons for my visitors, please."

Mavis reappeared soon after Pemberley returned, bringing the two factory visitors freshly starched caps and aprons. There was an apron for the factory owner, too, but his was dark blue and had his name embroidered across the front: *S. L. Lidcup*.

"Have you tried my jams before?" he asked as he tied his apron.

"We have indeed, Mr Lidcup, and they're very good indeed," said Churchill.

"Excellent! That's just what I like to hear. We're making a rather excellent plum jam today. Come and have a look!"

Over the next twenty minutes, he proudly showed Churchill and Pemberley how the jam was made. "I refer to my ladies as Lidcup's Angels!" he announced as they watched lines of female workers sorting plums in long wooden troughs.

At the next stage, the ladies wielded little knives as they made deft cuts in the plums.

"The stones are removed from the fruit by hand," said Mr Lidcup, "but the chopping is done by machine these days. We have all the latest machinery here! This is Sylvia. She's a master of the chopping machine."

Sylvia gave them a broad smile and continued with her work.

Churchill's favourite section was the one in which the fruit was boiled up in large copper vats. Each had one lady stirring the mixture while another poured in powdery sugar from large bags. "Looking good, Lily!" Mr Lidcup said encouragingly with a grin.

The clank of jars grew louder as they approached the final section.

"The finished product!" announced the factory owner as jam-filled jars were shunted toward noisy machines where the lids were pressed on. "The jam is almost ready for the shop shelves. Isn't that right, Barnaby?"

One of the few men who appeared to work in the factory, Barnaby nodded and carefully glued a label onto a jar. Then Mr Lidcup picked it up and presented it to Churchill.

"Now all you need is a freshly baked and buttered slice of bread to spread that on, don't you think?"

Although it had only been an hour since breakfast, Churchill's stomach rumbled at the thought. "Oh, very much so. Thank you, Mr Lidcup."

A short while later, Mavis relieved the two ladies of their caps and aprons.

"Thank you very much for the tour of your factory, Mr Lidcup," said Churchill. "It has been most enjoyable."

"The pleasure was all mine," he responded with a slight bow.

Churchill wondered if his mood would change when she mentioned Mr Spooner. "We were very sorry to hear about the sad passing of your brother-in-law," she ventured.

His face fell. "Awfully sad, isn't it? I've sent my commiserations to Edwina, but I don't suppose she'll be grateful for them."

"Why not?"

"Jeremy and I didn't see eye to eye, unfortunately. But that's a story for another day."

"Oh, we'd be more than happy to hear it now. My assistant and I are private detectives and we have Mrs Spooner's blessing to investigate her husband's murder."

His face fell even further. "Is that the real reason you're here? You weren't really interested in my factory at all, were you?"

"We're exceptionally interested in your factory and your jam, Mr Lidcup! And we're enormously grateful for the time you've taken to show us around today. Make no bones about it, I shall be recommending your preserves to everybody I meet from this day forth."

"But you'd also like to find out more about my brother-in-law?"

"Yes, we would."

"And you're trying to track down the murderer?"

"We are indeed."

He checked his watch. "Well, I suppose I can spare another five minutes. Jeremy may have disliked me enormously, but I'm still keen to do all I can to help find the person who dropped that enormous bell on his head. Dreadful business! Let's go and talk in my office."

Mr Lidcup's office was situated in a corner of the factory that was raised up on stilts so he could look out over the factory floor from his window. Accessible via a small flight of steps, it was cosy inside with comfortable seating and a little electrical fire for warmth.

As she sat down, Churchill glanced over at the desk, hoping to see the handwritten plum jam recipe that had been stolen from Mr Spooner's dining table. To her great disappointment, the desk was clean and tidy. Mr Lidcup did not appear to be someone who left things lying about.

"Mavis will bring us tea," said the factory owner as he took a seat behind his desk. "Now, where were we?"

"You mentioned that Edwina Spooner wouldn't have been grateful for your commiserations following the death of her husband."

"Ah, yes. It's dreadfully sad that I've been unable to express my condolences in person. All I can do is mourn poor Jeremy's passing from afar. Between you and me, Mrs Churchill, and the delightful Miss Pemberley of course, it's all based on a terrible misunderstanding."

"How so?"

"This jam factory was left to my dear wife, Jemima, by her adorable father. My wife sadly died ten years ago, but I have continued to run the place as best I can. It's a lot of work, and I can't deny the fact that it has felt like a millstone around my neck at times. Jeremy was Jemima's brother, and he was very bitter about the fact that Jemima had inherited the factory. I think he'd hoped it would be his, you see."

"It's quite unusual for a factory to pass to the daughter rather than the son."

"Yes, undoubtedly so. But Mr Spooner Senior was quite insistent that Jemima take it on. She had a natural penchant for jam, you see. I can't say that I shared it. Jam? I had no interest in jam!" He spread his palms and laughed. "I come from a family of bookkeepers. Pens and ledgers were my thing. But I was deeply in love with my dear, departed wife… and if she came with a jam factory, well, that had to be my burden."

"How very noble of you, Mr Lidcup."

"Oh, I don't consider myself noble." He gave a humble shrug. "Just a chap who was hopelessly in love."

Churchill felt her toes curl.

"Jeremy Spooner was a good man," he continued. "It's a shame he became so embittered by life's circumstances. A bit of a waste, wouldn't you say? Why spend one's years bemoaning what might have happened when you have the rest of your life to be getting on with?"

"A very valid sentiment, Mr Lidcup. When we spoke with Mrs Spooner, she mentioned that his plum jam recipe had been stolen."

"Is that so? I recall that Jeremy enjoyed making jam. Only natural, I suppose, coming from a jam-making family as he did."

"I hope you don't mind me telling you this, Mr Lidcup, and I sincerely hope you aren't upset by the allegation, but Mrs Spooner suggested that you had perhaps taken the recipe."

The factory owner threw his head back and laughed loudly. "That old chestnut! I'd heard that Jeremy was in possession of an old recipe that had been passed down through generations of Spooners. He was extremely protective of it, apparently, and completely preoccupied with the idea that I would one day snatch it from him. I even heard the old chap kept it locked away in a drawer! But I can assure you, Mrs Churchill, that I have never seen it, nor have I ever had any interest in doing so. We have a very modern way of making jam these days, as you've seen, so why should I be interested in some old, sticky recipe? I suppose it was the one thing Jeremy had that he thought I didn't have. Poor chap. You have to feel sorry for him, really. Or *had* to, I should say. Ah, Mavis! Here's the tea."

Mavis set the tea tray down on his desk before leaving the room.

"Mrs Spooner informed us that the recipe wasn't locked away in a drawer at the time of its disappearance. It was actually lying on the dining table beside an open window," said Churchill.

"On that busy lane? But anybody could have slipped their hand in and grabbed the recipe!"

"That's exactly what she believes to have happened."

"If anybody wanted it, that is. I suppose someone might have been intrigued to see what it was and snatched it, then swiftly realised it was just a dull, dog-eared jam recipe and thrown it away. It's wrong for anybody to go putting their hands through windows and snatching things off tables, of course, but we must accept that some people are inclined to do such things. Mrs Spooner thinks it was me, does she?"

"Yes."

"Do I look like the sort of chap who goes around poking his hands through open windows to snatch bits of paper left lying on dining tables? Me? A busy factory owner? I'm sure you'll agree that I have far better things to do, Mrs Churchill. It was rather foolish of the old chap to leave it lying there in the first place, though. If it was as precious as he said it was, why wasn't it locked away?"

"He was picking plums in the orchard at the time."

"Well, one does need something to make the jam with, doesn't one? But even if he was out picking plums, he should have kept the recipe in a safe place. Although I suppose there are plenty of other jam recipes he could have used if it went missing." Mr Lidcup picked up the teapot and began pouring out the tea.

"You know nothing at all about the missing recipe then, Mr Lidcup?"

"Absolutely nothing, Mrs Churchill. It's a dreadful shame that, in the depths of her grief, Mrs Spooner is holding on to the mistaken belief that I was somehow interested in that jam recipe. What on earth does any of this have to do with the poor chap's murder, anyway? I'd like to know who dropped that bell on his head, and I think Mrs Spooner should be thinking along the same lines rather than casting aspersions on me."

"Mr Spooner can't have been murdered for the recipe because it went missing before his death. There is a suggestion that he was murdered to keep him quiet about something. Would you happen to know anything about that?"

"Why should I know anything about that?"

"It's possible that someone wanted him silenced."

"That wouldn't be enormously surprising, the way he used to carry on with those bells. They practically shook us out of our beds every Sunday morning! Not to mention the evening practices. They went on and on and on. Tea?"

"Thank you, Mr Lidcup."

He handed Churchill and Pemberley their cups.

"Just out of interest, Mr Lidcup, do you have your own special jam recipes?"

"Of course. They're extremely special, and well-guarded, too, I might add." He pointed to a safe in the corner of his office. "They're all kept in there, for my eyes only."

"Nobody else sees the recipes?"

"No, just me. I have collected them over the many years I've spent in the business. I can understand why Jeremy was a little protective of his family recipe, even though no one else was the least bit interested in it. My own recipes are far more important given that an entire business depends on them!"

"How has business been recently, Mr Lidcup?"

"Excellent, as always. I supply all sorts of places: shops, hotels, tea rooms and the like. Only last week I struck up a deal to supply a shop in Honiton. That's in Devon, which means we're finally expanding our reach beyond the borders of Dorset! Isn't that wonderful? I've also had some interest from a lady who runs some large tea rooms in Somerset. All very interesting, wouldn't you say? And as for this latest batch of plum jam… Well, it's rather different from our last. It'll blow your socks off, if you don't mind me saying so, Mrs Churchill."

"That would be rather interesting."

"It would, wouldn't it?" He winked. "I'd better drink up. I need to get back out on the factory floor. It boosts morale when I'm out there with the troops."

Chapter 18

"What did you think of Mr Lidcup, Mrs Churchill?" asked Pemberley as the two ladies and their dog walked out through the tall factory gates and continued on past a little row of shops.

"A bit smooth, wouldn't you say?"

"Decidedly smooth."

"Too eager to create a good impression and gain our approval, I reckon."

"Suspiciously so?"

"Very suspiciously so. But if he knew that Mr Spooner was planning to have something published in the *Compton Poppleford Gazette*, I'd like to know how."

"Could Smithy Miggins have told Mr Lidcup?"

"I don't think he'd have done that. He seemed very keen to keep Mr Spooner's confidence."

"Until you plied him with scrumpy after Mr Spooner died."

"Well, yes. But I believe he would only ever have been willing to reveal Mr Spooner's secret under those two conditions. We need to work out who else might have told

Mr Lidcup about the planned article." Churchill paused beside a rusty water pump. "How do we get to Hyacinth Lane from here?"

"Oh, that's easy. Just follow me."

They strolled along a little winding street and found Hyacinth Lane, where Mrs Spooner lived. The lane's old, tiled roofs sloped at varying angles and the houses' beamed upper storeys jutted out over the pavement. They passed small, low doorways and crooked, mullioned windows. Colourful pots and baskets of flowers nestled beside doorways. A horse and cart plodded up the cobbled lane and a delivery boy bounced past on his bicycle.

"Which number does Mrs Spooner live at?" asked Churchill.

"I don't know. She did say that Mr Lidcup's lady friend, Miss Harpum, lives close by at Tulip Cottage. And I suppose we're looking for a window that opens out onto the lane."

"Ah yes, the famous dining room window. There are quite a lot of windows overlooking this lane. Look at this one here." Churchill stopped. "The curtains are drawn." She stepped back and looked at the cottage's other windows. "All the curtains here are drawn. A recent death in the family, perhaps?"

"Or someone's feeling rather lazy today."

"I think it must be Mrs Spooner's cottage. Let's knock."

Mrs Spooner answered the door, her face woeful.

"We're so sorry to disturb you again," said Churchill, "but we have a couple more questions if you don't mind answering them."

"I'd be very happy to," she replied sadly. "Anything to find out who killed my husband. Come in."

The interior of the cottage was lit with a dim lamp, and Churchill could just make out the outlines of furniture in the gloom. She fought the urge to fling open the curtains, moving awkwardly with her hands stretched out in front of her to find somewhere to sit.

"We're particularly interested in the jam recipe that was taken from your dining table," she said, sinking into a saggy cushioned chair. "Are you able to tell me exactly when the theft occurred?"

There was no response.

"Mrs Spooner?" Churchill said, addressing the shadowy figure in the chair opposite her.

"I don't think she's here," said Pemberley.

"Oh, it's you in that chair! Where's Mrs Spooner gone?"

"I don't know."

"Shall I open the curtains a bit?" said a voice from the doorway. "I've just realised how dark it is in here."

"Open them a lot if you like," said Churchill. "I'm sure your dearly departed husband wouldn't mind."

"No, I don't suppose he would."

Churchill waited impatiently as Mrs Spooner tugged the heavy curtains open.

"Is that better?" their host eventually asked.

"Much better."

"Oh, there's a dog in here! I wonder how it got in. That'll teach me to sit around in the dark. Get out of here! Shoo!"

"The dog belongs to us, Mrs Spooner."

Pemberley picked Oswald up and held him protectively.

"Oh, I am sorry."

"Now, when was the recipe stolen?" asked Churchill.

Mrs Spooner sat down on the settee and gave this some thought. "I suppose it was about two weeks ago."

"About a week before your husband died?"

"Yes, I suppose it would have been about then."

"Can you remember which day of the week it was?"

She thought some more. "Tuesday, I think."

"Are you quite sure about that?"

Mrs Spooner reflected again. "Oh, I don't know now. Perhaps it was the Wednesday." She chewed her lower lip as she pondered. "No, it was definitely the Tuesday. We had a chicken pie that lunchtime."

"Do you have chicken pie every Tuesday lunchtime?"

"Yes, we do… or rather *did*. I can't say I'm in the mood to make it at the moment."

"Perfectly understandable, Mrs Spooner. Are you quite sure you had chicken pie that lunchtime?"

"Yes, because there was some left over, and it was on the dining table cooling down with the recipe lying next to it. Jeremy had mentioned while we were eating that he intended to go to the orchard to pick some plums, so it was after we'd finished eating that he fetched the recipe and placed it next to the remains of the pie in its dish."

"What time do you think the recipe was taken?"

"We must have had our chicken pie at twelve o'clock, because we always ate at that time. I should think he went out to the orchard at about one o'clock."

"How long was he there for?"

"Well, it's a ten-minute walk, and he came back with a fair amount of fruit. I don't think he'd have been back within the hour. I'd say it was likely to have been around half-past two."

"And that's when he discovered that the recipe was missing?"

"Yes, as soon as he got back. He said, 'Someone's taken my recipe!' And then he fell into a dreadful panic."

"It's safe to say, then, Mrs Spooner, that the recipe was taken at some point between one o'clock and half-past two on the Tuesday?"

"Yes, that would be about right."

"You were in the house at the time, were you not?"

"Yes, I was here all the time. That's why we weren't too worried about the window being left open. We would have closed it if we'd both gone out."

"Were you in the dining room at any time while your husband was out picking plums?"

"No. I was out in the garden pruning the roses."

"Someone was able to take that recipe between one and half-past two that day without anybody noticing because you weren't in the dining room at any point during that time. Is that right?"

"Yes, that's right. How I wish I had been! And how I wish Jeremy hadn't left it lying there on the table!"

"Thank you, Mrs Spooner. You've been extremely helpful. With this new information we can look for witnesses who may have seen whoever it was that took the recipe."

"It was Mr Lidcup."

"Very likely, but it'll help us enormously if we can find someone who actually saw him. Would you mind opening the dining room window to the same point as it was on that fateful day? If you could also place a sheet of paper on the table in the same position as the recipe, that would be most helpful."

The two ladies and Oswald left the Spooner house and stood out on the lane beside the dining room window.

Churchill peered in through the open window and gazed at the sheet of paper on the table. "It's easy to see how someone might have slipped their arm in through here and snatched the recipe up off the table." She stepped up to the open window and reached in to grab the piece of paper. She was just about to pick it up when she felt a sharp stinging sensation across her knuckles.

"No you don't! Not this time!"

"Ow!" Churchill clasped her sore hand and peered in through the window.

Mrs Spooner stood on the other side with a clenched jaw and a knitting needle in her hand. "Oh, Mrs Churchill!" she exclaimed, her face aghast. "It's you!" She lowered the knitting needle.

"Of course it's me! Who did you think it was?"

"I had no idea! I decided I'd better be on my guard these days."

"It was just me recreating the scene of the crime."

"Oh, that's what you were doing."

"Yes." Churchill rubbed her hand again. "We're just heading off to find some witnesses."

Chapter 19

"I'M BEGINNING to wonder whether Mrs Spooner has bats in the belfry," muttered Churchill as they crossed the road toward a little jumble of cottages. "Did you see how she attacked me with that knitting needle?"

"She's a grieving widow, and she's probably feeling extra vigilant after her recent tragedy."

"True. Still no excuse, though."

They called at the door of the cottage opposite Mrs Spooner's home and spoke to a small, sharp-featured lady.

"We're investigating the theft of a jam recipe from the house across the road," said Churchill.

"Ah, yes. Mr and Mrs Spooner."

"You've no doubt heard about Mr Spooner's tragic death. We're particularly interested in the theft of his secret jam recipe, which occurred on Tuesday the third of this month between the times of one and half-past two in the afternoon. We're interested to know whether you saw anybody outside the house at that time. Lingering, perhaps. Maybe even putting their arm through an open window."

"No, I didn't see anyone."

"Were you at home at that time?"

"I can't remember now."

"I see. It was a Tuesday, early afternoon. Are you usually home at that time?"

"Yes, usually. But if I was here, I certainly wasn't looking out of the window and noticing anything like that."

Churchill thanked the sharp-faced lady and they moved on to the next house. The door was eventually opened by a tired-looking young woman with hair falling into her face. Three small children squeezed past her and burst out into the street.

"Doggy!" they cried out, skipping past Churchill and Pemberley to pat Oswald on the head.

"Look out for motor cars!" their mother called out. "You can't jus' go runnin' out into the road like that!" She gave Churchill and Pemberley an exasperated look and wiped her brow with her apron. "'Ow can I 'elp?"

Churchill repeated the same questions she had asked the sharp-faced lady in the neighbouring house.

"I didn't see nothin'," replied the young woman. "Don't get a chance to notice nothin' these days." As she spoke, another small child squeezed past her and dashed out into the street. "Mind out for motor cars!" she shouted again. She turned back to Churchill and Pemberley. "'Ow comes they never listen?"

Churchill shrugged. "I think that's children for you," she concluded unhelpfully. "You're absolutely sure you didn't see anything that Tuesday? We're really quite keen to find out who stole Mr Spooner's secret jam recipe."

"Don't suppose it matters to 'im no more, does it?"

"It matters to his widow."

"Oh, right. S'pose it does. Thinkin' about it, there was summat odd 'appened out 'ere not so long ago. Might of been the Tuesday. All I remember's little Millie come runnin' back in 'ere with a bag o' sweets."

"That's unusual, is it?"

"Yeah, 'cause I 'ad no idea where she'd got 'em from. An' then she told me a nice man 'ad gave 'em to 'er."

"Oh dear. That doesn't sound good. How old is your Millie?"

"She's five. Might be six now, come ter think about it. I lose count of 'em sometimes."

"Did she tell you anything else about this 'nice man'?"

"'E was tall. That's what she told me. Said a tall man 'ad given 'er some sweets and asked 'er not to say nothin'."

Churchill shuddered. "Did she mention anything else?" she reluctantly asked.

"I asked 'er what 'e didn't want 'er to say nothin' about," replied the woman, "an' she told me 'e'd been pokin' 'is arm in through some winda."

Churchill smiled. "Is that so? Mr and Mrs Spooner's window, perchance?"

"Must of been. She pointed over there. Said she'd been playin' in the lane when a tall man put 'is arm in through the winda of that 'ouse. Told me she'd been watchin' 'im, 'cause she thought it weren't a good thing to be doin'. When 'e noticed 'er watchin', 'e smiled and said 'e'd be back in a minute. Sure enough, 'e come back with a bag of sweets he must of bought from Miss Gurney's sweet shop. That's when 'e's told Millie not to say nothin'."

"And the good child completely ignored his instructions, of course," replied Churchill. "Are you familiar with Mr Lidcup, the jam factory owner?"

"No, but me auntie used to work there."

"Used to?"

"She left 'cause she didn't like 'im. You think it was 'im pokin' 'is 'and in through the winda, do yer?"

"It's a possibility. What we need to do is find a photograph of Mr Lidcup, show it to little Millie and ask her if he is the 'nice man' who bought her the sweets. Would you mind if we did that?"

"I don't mind."

"Wonderful. May I ask your name?"

"Mrs Pugh."

"Thank you, Mrs Pugh. We'll be back as soon as we can find a photograph of Mr Lidcup."

"Pleased to be of 'elp."

"I'd also be interested to speak to your aunt about Mr Lidcup. Would you mind telling us where we can find her?"

"Me Auntie Pam's two doors down. Mrs Mullard, 'er name is."

"Forty years of service I gave that man! Forty long years of pipping, chopping, boiling, filling and capping." White-haired Mrs Mullard had plenty to say for herself once Churchill had mentioned Mr Lidcup's name. She stood on her well-scrubbed doorstep, arms folded across her large bosom. "I was one of the original Lidcup Angels," she continued. "That's what they call the girls at the jam factory. Only once you pass thirty you're no longer an angel."

"What are you then?"

"Nothing. Just a jam worker."

"A Lidcup Matron?" suggested Pemberley.

"What's that, Miss Pemberley?" said Churchill.

"That's what Lidcup Angels should become when they're over thirty. Lidcup Matrons. It has a nice ring to it."

"Perhaps you could suggest it to Mr Lidcup. In the

meantime, let's try to get to the bottom of this stolen jam recipe, shall we?"

"Stolen another one, has he?" said Mrs Mullard. "That doesn't surprise me one bit."

Churchill's interest was piqued. "He's done it before?"

"Every jam he's turned out of that factory is from a stolen recipe."

"Good grief!"

"I tell a lie. The first batch wasn't from a stolen recipe; it was one he'd come up with himself. But to be quite honest with you, it was horrible. It really stuck to the roof of your mouth."

"Oh dear."

"He nearly went out of business, it was so awful. Then he stole a recipe from somewhere, and hey presto! Everyone liked his jam."

"This is very interesting indeed, Mrs Mullard. We have reason to believe he stole a plum jam recipe from your neighbour, Mr Spooner."

"That poor chap over the road? Spooner was his brother-in-law, wasn't he? It wouldn't surprise me if he stole a recipe from him. Lidcup would steal his own grandmother's recipes given half a chance. In fact, he probably already has done."

"Did you see Mr Lidcup stealing Mr Spooner's recipe about two weeks ago? He put his arm in through the open window and took it."

"No, I didn't see that. But I don't need to have seen it to know that it happened. It's just the sort of thing he'd do."

"Thank you, Mrs Mullard. You've been most helpful."

Chapter 20

"What do you want from me now?" asked Smithy Miggins when Churchill and Pemberley approached him outside the offices of the *Compton Poppleford Gazette*.

"A photograph," replied Churchill.

"A photograph of what?" He puffed out a cloud of tobacco smoke.

"I'm assuming your newspaper has a library of photographs of the great and the good of Compton Poppleford."

"It does. What are you after?"

"A photograph of Mr Lidcup, the jam factory owner. We only need to borrow it to show it to a witness who claims to have seen him poking his arm in through Mr Spooner's dining room window at the time the jam recipe was stolen."

His eyebrows shot up. "That's very interesting indeed. Who's the witness?"

"We don't reveal our sources. Remember, Mr Miggins? We'll return the photograph as soon as we're done."

He considered this for a moment while puffing on his cigarette.

"A prompt answer would be helpful, Mr Miggins."

"I'm just trying to work out what's in it for me."

"Practically nothing. But does there always need to be something in it for you?"

"That's the way I like to do things."

"How about a nicely solved murder to write about once I've concluded my investigation?"

He laughed. "I suppose I'll have to be content with that. I'll go and fetch it."

Smithy Miggins stepped inside the office, then returned a moment later with the photograph and handed it to Churchill.

"Having met the man himself, I'd say this photograph flatters him a little," she commented. "He doesn't look like a jam factory owner at all. He's trying to look like one of those Hollywood actors."

"Douglas Fairbanks," added Pemberley, peering over Churchill's shoulder. "That's who he's trying to look like."

"Yes, I can see why you might say that," replied Churchill, turning the photograph one way and then the other. "Isn't it clever what a bit of good lighting can achieve? Does this have the photographic studio's name on it? Oh yes, it has. I shall make a note of it."

"Reckon they'll be able to make you look like Mary Pickford?" chuckled the news reporter.

"You may laugh now, Mr Miggins, but I closely resembled her in my youth. I'll have you know that I turned many a young man's head back then."

"That's nice to know, Mrs Churchill. Do let me know what your witness says."

"I certainly shall. Just a quick question, if I may. Did

you happen to mention Mr Spooner's secret to anyone else?"

"No."

"Are you absolutely sure about that?"

"Yes."

"I'm wondering if Mr Lidcup found out that Mr Spooner intended to have something about the stolen recipe published."

"Beats me." He spread his hands to confirm his ignorance.

"You didn't mention it to anyone at all?"

"Only Mr Trollope."

"Ah, yes." Churchill had encountered the hatchet-faced editor of the *Gazette* while investigating the death of Mrs Furzgate at the Piddleton Hotel. "Is it possible that Mr Trollope might have mentioned the impending article to Mr Lidcup?"

"Absolutely not! A respectable newspaper editor would never do such a thing!"

The two ladies and their dog returned to Mrs Pugh's house and were shown into a small, cosy room filled with noisy, excitable children. Oswald soon became the focus of their attention and Churchill noticed that Mrs Pugh's hair had fallen into an even more noticeable state of disarray.

Churchill showed her the photograph of Mr Lidcup.

"Flatters 'im a bit, don't it?" she commented.

"That's exactly what we thought. Do you think your Millie would be happy to take a look at this and confirm whether he's the one who gave her the sweets?"

Mrs Pugh nodded. "I'll ask 'er."

She extracted a small girl from the noisy group and presented her to Churchill and Pemberley. Millie glanced up at them with her large blue eyes, then shoved her fingers into her mouth.

"Take yer fingers out yer mouth, Millie," said her mother.

The girl refused with a resolute shake of her head.

"Sorry, Mrs Churchill, she does that when she's feeling shy."

"No matter," replied Churchill. "The important thing is whether she recognises the man in the photograph or not."

"These nice ladies are goin' to show you a photograph, Millie," said her mother. "They want you to tell 'em if this man's the same one you saw puttin' 'is arm through Mr Spooner's window. The man what bought you them sweets. D'you remember?"

The girl nodded, her eyes fixed on Churchill.

"Hello there, Millie," said Churchill as kindly as she knew how.

She held out the photograph and the little girl glanced at it, then chewed on her fingers once again.

"Is this the man who bought you the bag of sweets, Millie?" asked Churchill.

The little girl said nothing.

"The man who put his arm in through the window, then bought you the sweets and asked you not to say anything?" Churchill probed.

The little girl gave an almost imperceptible nod.

"Take yer fingers out yer mouth, Millie," instructed her mother, "and speak ter the lady politely."

The little girl turned away and hung her head.

"Judging by her reaction, Mrs Pugh, would you say that Millie recognises this man?"

"I think so. She's a bit shy." She turned to her daughter again. "Millie, can yer tell us if that's the same man?"

The girl gave a little nod, her back still turned to Churchill and Pemberley.

Mrs Pugh sighed. "'Eavens above, Millie! Just turn round and tell the two ladies!"

The little girl turned to face Churchill and Pemberley again. "Yeth," she muttered through her mouthful of fingers.

"I'm afraid that's all yer gonna get, Mrs Churchill."

"That's quite all right. If you're satisfied that she recognised the man in the photograph, so are we."

"She seemed to. 'Asn't said no, 'as she?"

"Very interesting indeed, wouldn't you say?" said Churchill as the two ladies walked along Hyacinth Lane. "Everything points to Mr Lidcup so far. I think it's about time we informed Inspector Mappin of our findings."

"Oh, no. Must we?"

"I realise we're the ones who've done all the hard work, Pembers, but it's only reasonable that such a strong suspicion should be reported to the local constabulary."

Chapter 21

"Sorry to interrupt your tea break, Inspector Mappin, but we have important news."

"Tea break?" retorted the brown-whiskered inspector as he swiftly removed his feet from his desk. "I don't take tea breaks while I'm on duty!" He closed the lid of the biscuit tin, pushed a cup and saucer to the edge of the desk and dusted some crumbs from his uniform. "Refreshments," he added. "I have *refreshments* while I'm working. Never an actual tea break!"

"We didn't come here to discuss your working practices, Inspector. We've come to say that it's quite obvious to us who was behind the murder of Mr Spooner."

"Oh, yes. You don't need to tell me that, Mrs Churchill. And before you ask… I shall arrest him as soon as a crucial piece of evidence is found. He's already been interviewed by myself a number of times."

"You don't say! That certainly sounds promising, Inspector. Can I just check that we're talking about the same man?"

"No need to check. I should think it's quite obvious

even to those with the tiniest of brains that Mr Whiplark carried out the atrocity."

"I feared we might have different suspects in mind."

"He's the *only* possible suspect, Mrs Churchill! And if you're here to tell me differently, I shall have to put an end to such time-wasting conversation before it's begun."

"So you can continue with your tea break in peace?"

"*Refreshments!* It *wasn't* a tea break. Go on, then. Who's your suspect?"

"I don't think I shall tell you after all, Inspector. I fear you'll merely want to put an end to the time-wasting conversation, given that you're so uninterested."

"I'm at least a bit interested to find out what, or whom, you've come up with, Mrs Churchill."

"So you are interested?"

"A little bit."

"Very well, then. It's Mr Lidcup, owner of the jam factory."

"Mr Lidcup?! Why on earth would Mr Lidcup want to murder Mr Spooner? For one thing, he's a member of Mr Spooner's family, and for another he's a highly respected local businessman."

"That doesn't mean he's not a murderer."

"Preposterous! Where on earth did you get such a notion?"

"Through our conversations with many people in recent days. You're aware, I suppose, of the long-running feud between Mr Lidcup and Mr Spooner?"

"Yes, I'm aware that there was some ill-feeling."

"And Mr Spooner's secret jam recipe was stolen. His widow told us her late husband believed Mr Lidcup had taken it. This story is backed up by a news reporter from the *Compton Poppleford Gazette*—"

"Smithy Miggins, no doubt."

"I prefer not to reveal my sources. But this reporter said that Mr Spooner approached him with regard to writing an article about his secret jam recipe being stolen by the owner of a jam factory."

Inspector Mappin put his head in his hands. "What silly nonsense. Why would Mr Lidcup bother to steal an old jam recipe?"

"We have a witness who saw him take it."

"Really?"

"Yes. It may be worth your while speaking to her." Churchill thought of the young girl with her fingers crammed into her mouth and wondered whether Inspector Mappin might have more success in speaking to her than she had.

"I could try, I suppose." He took out his notebook and pencil. "Perhaps you could give me the name and address just in case I get round to it."

"Her name is Millie Pugh and she lives in the cottage opposite Mrs Spooner's. She was playing out in the street when—"

"I'm sorry. Did you say she was playing out in the street?"

"Yes. She was playing out in the street when Mr Lidcup came along and put his arm through Mr and Mrs Spooner's open window and took the recipe. Then he bought the young girl some sweets and asked her not to say anything."

"How old is Millie Pugh?"

"Five."

Inspector Mappin snapped his notebook shut. "A five-year-old child is not a valid witness, Mrs Churchill."

"She may not be as reliable as a fully grown adult, but then we're not expecting her to speak in a court of law, are we? Having said that, there's no doubting what the child saw. We showed her a photograph of Mr Lidcup and she confirmed that he was the man she had seen taking the recipe."

"Children can be very fanciful, Mrs Churchill! They have vivid imaginations. And they'll often say whatever they think an adult wants to hear."

"We've also spoken to a disgruntled former employee who told us Mr Lidcup was known for stealing jam recipes."

"That's exactly the sort of thing you'd expect to hear from a disgruntled former employee! They rarely have anything nice to say, do they?"

"Surely all this is enough to warrant you visiting the jam factory and asking to see the contents of Mr Lidcup's safe, Inspector. That's where he stores all his jam recipes. I'm absolutely certain Mr Spooner's recipe will be among them."

"I can't go marching about asking to look inside people's safes on the basis of a young child's say so. It's just not how these things work, Mrs Churchill. And even if Mr Lidcup did steal the recipe, why would he have wanted to murder Mr Spooner?"

"To silence him. My source at the *Compton Poppleford Gazette* had agreed to meet with Mr Spooner a second time to discuss the article. Unfortunately, Mr Spooner was murdered before that could happen. Interesting, don't you think?"

"So you're saying, Mrs Churchill, that Mr Lidcup murdered Mr Spooner because he didn't want anybody to know he had stolen Mr Spooner's secret jam recipe."

"That's exactly what I'm saying!"

Inspector Mappin shook his head. "I really can't believe that a successful, generous, popular local factory owner would sink to such depths. I've known Mr Lidcup a long time, and it would be completely out of character for him. He has far more important work to be getting on with, and everyone knows he fell out with his brother-in-law a long time ago."

"Am I right in thinking that Mr Lidcup is a good friend of yours, Inspector?"

"We play tennis together."

"Might you perhaps be a little biased in his favour?"

"Now, look here, Mrs Churchill! I never allow personal friendships to interfere with my work. I've lived in this village all my life, and I'm on good terms with practically everyone who lives in it. That said, I still need to be able to lay down the law when incidents like this arise. And if that means apprehending a friend who I believe has committed a crime, then so be it. I'd have no qualms about doing so."

"But you have no interest in finding out whether Mr Lidcup has the stolen recipe or not?"

He sighed. "I don't suppose there would be any harm in me asking him about it, but I shall take him at his word if he denies the theft."

"Take him at his word? Why on earth would you do that? Why not simply ask to look inside his safe?"

"I'll take him at his word because he's a man of his word. And if he assures me he didn't steal the recipe, it'll be very difficult indeed for me to go looking inside his safe."

"Inspector, all you need to do is ask if you can take a look. If he's willing to help with the investigation, I can't see why he would be resistant to the idea."

Inspector Mappin got up from his seat. "That's quite enough, Mrs Churchill! I do not appreciate you marching into my office and telling me how to do my job. The terrible murder of Mr Spooner is an ongoing police investigation, and I will only discuss the details with my colleagues; not some nosy old lady who's set herself up as a private detective on the high street. May I remind you that this case has nothing to do with you? I'd appreciate it if you kept your nose well out of it."

"We have Mrs Spooner's blessing to investigate her husband's death."

Inspector Mappin shook his head. "You've been haranguing his widow, have you?"

"Not at all. She seemed very grateful for our help."

"Poor woman." He walked over to his hatstand and put on his hat. "Do excuse me, ladies. I've important work to be getting on with. The sooner I can gather this vital piece of evidence against Mr Whiplark the better."

"You're certain he murdered Mr Spooner, are you?"

"Absolutely certain. So there's really no need for you to be meddling with this case anymore, Mrs Churchill. We almost have our man."

Chapter 22

"This case is becoming exceedingly frustrating," said Churchill once she and Pemberley were back at their office. "It's like trying to clamber up a greasy pole."

"Ugh! I had to do that once."

"When?"

"While I was visiting Chile with the lady of international travel. It was part of a competition we were having with the locals."

"And how did you fare?"

"Quite well, actually. Ouch!"

"Pricked yourself again, Pembers?"

"Yes. I really don't like needles."

"Which is why your insistence on making that prayer cushion continues to baffle me."

"I've nearly finished one side now, but it's taking me a long time and I still haven't finished *The Havana Heist*. Perhaps you could read a chapter aloud to me while I work."

"I'm far too busy for that sort of thing, Pembers. I'm trying to work out how we can take a look inside

Mr Lidcup's safe." Churchill bit into her second eclair.

"If we were Lightfinger Jones in *The Havana Heist,* we'd just break in."

"Which would be both impossible and illegal. People in books seem to get away with all sorts don't they? Did I just hear someone on our stairs? Oh golly, I do hope it's not Mrs Higginbath again! I'd forgotten all about her naughty ornament."

The footsteps grew louder. Then, to Churchill's great relief, the door was pushed open by a morose-looking lady with a drawn face and dark clothing.

"Mrs Spooner!" Churchill stood and drew up a chair for the widow. "Do make yourself comfortable. How are you faring?"

"I'm not, really."

"Quite understandable."

"I came to find out how your investigation is progressing."

"The good news is, we have a suspect."

"Oh, good!"

"The bad news is, Inspector Mappin is convinced that the culprit is someone else entirely."

"Oh. So who do you think did it?"

"Mr Lidcup."

"And what about Inspector Mappin?"

"He's certain that it was Mr Whiplark."

She nodded slowly. "Neither is implausible. Perhaps they both did it. Maybe Mr Lidcup and Mr Whiplark were in cahoots."

"Not an impossibility, I suppose, but at the present time we've at something of an impasse."

"What's that?"

"Just a little puzzle about what to do next. Would you

like some tea, Mrs Spooner?"

"No, thank you."

"Chocolate eclair?"

"No, thank you."

"All I can suggest, Mrs Spooner, is that you speak to Inspector Mappin yourself, and try to persuade him to look inside Mr Lidcup's safe for the stolen jam recipe. I've tried myself, but he wouldn't listen. It's awfully frustrating. If only we could just go in there and grab it. That would solve everything, wouldn't it?"

"It would, and it would vindicate my poor Jeremy as well. How he suffered when he realised his recipe had disappeared! And he immediately knew that his brother-in-law had taken it. Who else would have been interested in doing so?"

"Who else indeed?"

"I so appreciate your help, Mrs Churchill. I know you're not interested in receiving any sort of payment, but I do have a little money I could give you in return for all your trouble."

"I won't hear of it, Mrs Spooner. I told you from the outset that I was only interested in solving the case. The satisfaction of catching the murderer will be enough for me. However, I must reluctantly admit that I've reached a dead end on this occasion. I really don't know what to do next."

"I have seventy pounds…" began Mrs Spooner.

"Seventy pounds? I won't hear it. You keep your money, Mrs Spooner, and I'll see what we can do next. Having a little break and a think in these cases often yields new ideas."

"Well, please consider the seventy pounds, Mrs Churchill. Just in case you need to pay anyone else for their help."

"That's very kind of you, Mrs Spooner."

The widow rose up out of her seat. "I'd better get back. I need to make sure everything's ready for Jeremy's funeral tomorrow."

"I wish you the very best of luck with that, Mrs Spooner."

"I keep wondering if *she'll* be there."

"Who?"

"I don't know her name."

"Whose name?"

"The lady Jeremy was… Oh dear. I don't like to speak ill of him now that he's gone."

"I'm sure you'd never do that. The lady Jeremy was…?"

Mrs Spooner returned to her chair and lowered her voice. "He had a lady friend. He didn't know I knew, but there were certain signs."

"There usually are."

"Lipstick stains on his collar, unexplained outings… that sort of thing."

"But you never found out who she was?"

"No, and I never asked him. I didn't know how to… But I think she must have been a doctor's secretary."

"What makes you think that?"

"After Jeremy passed away, I did some tidying in his shed and found a handbag tucked in behind the work-bench. It had a few personal items in it: boiled sweets, a handkerchief and so on. There was nothing that gave much away about the owner's identity aside from a stethoscope."

"A stethoscope?"

"Yes. The thing doctors use to listen to your chest."

"Why would a doctor's secretary carry a stethoscope about with her?"

"I have no idea. Maybe the doctor left it lying about at the surgery, so she picked it up and put it in her handbag ready to return to him the next day. Although how the handbag found its way into Jeremy's shed, I really don't know."

"How very interesting, Mrs Spooner. The plot thickens!"

"Dr Richfield," said Churchill once Mrs Spooner had left. "He's the local doctor, isn't he?"

"Along with Dr Burkin."

"Two doctors. That means there must be two doctor's secretaries in the village."

"Dr Richfield and Dr Burkin share the same one."

"Who is she?"

"Miss Drumhead. The daughter of Farmer Drumhead."

"Might she have been Mr Spooner's paramour?"

"I very much doubt it. I've known Miss Drumhead since she was a tot, and I really can't imagine a young girl like her having any interest in Mr Spooner."

"It does seem unlikely. However, it's fair to assume that Mr Spooner's death will have caused his mistress to mourn. Perhaps she'll put in an appearance at the funeral, as Mrs Spooner suggested. It'll be a good place to look out for her. Perhaps she's a doctor's secretary from a village close by.

"In the meantime, I can feel another plan forming. I think it's time we consulted that shadowy acquaintance of yours, Mr Nightwalker, once again."

"His code name is Nightwalker. There's no 'Mr'."

"Well, you knew who I meant. What's the message we

need to put in the personal advertisement section of the *Gazette* to get his attention?"

"'Will Lady who took wrong umbrella from Butcher's Shop, Tuesday afternoon, kindly return?'"

"That's the one."

"What was it you wanted to ask him, Mrs Churchill?"

"We need some help, and Mrs Spooner has kindly offered us seventy pounds. All will become apparent, Pembers, once we've spoken with former Lidcup Angel Mrs Mullard again."

A short while later, Churchill and Pemberley were sitting in Mrs Mullard's front room and Churchill was busy explaining why she believed Mr Lidcup had murdered Mr Spooner.

"I can't say any of that surprises me," said the white-haired lady once Churchill had finished. "Lidcup's probably murdered more than just Spooner, if you ask me."

"Let's just concentrate on Mr Spooner's case for the time being. We need to get into Mr Lidcup's safe to see if the stolen jam recipe is in there."

"How are you going to do that?"

"Yes, how *are* we going to do that?" asked Pemberley.

"We'll have to sneak in somehow."

"You're going to break in?" asked Mrs Mullard.

"No, we're going to *sneak* in."

"What's the difference?"

"The difference is, we're not going to break anything."

"There are a lot of breakable things in that factory. All those jam jars, for a start."

"That's exactly why we're going to sneak in. Can you help us?"

Mrs Mullard folded her arms across her ample bosom.

"I'm not the sort of person who goes around sneaking into places, Mrs Churchill."

"Neither are we usually, but Miss Pemberley and I need to know how easy it would be to gain entry to the factory."

"You can just walk in there."

"I mean at night."

"At *night*?" exclaimed Pemberley, a concerned expression spreading across her face.

"You're actually planning to go in there at night?" asked Mrs Mullard.

"Yes."

"Do we have to?" queried Pemberley.

"Yes, Miss Pemberley! We need to get our hands on that recipe."

"But how are we going to do that? It's locked away in the safe."

"Then we need to find someone who knows how to break into safes."

"Such as?"

"That's what I'm hoping Mr Nightwalker can help us with."

"How are we going to get inside the building?"

"We'll ask if he knows of anyone who can pick locks, too."

"It sounds like an ambitious plan, Mrs Churchill," said Mrs Mullard, "but if you can find someone who knows how to pick locks and break open safes, perhaps you'll actually be able to pull it off."

"Only with a good deal of planning. You know the ins and outs of the place, Mrs Mullard. Would you help us come up with a plan?"

"I don't want to get myself in any trouble."

"You won't. Mr Lidcup will be the one who's in trouble at the end of all this. What do you say?"

"All right, then."

"Are we really going to break into the jam factory?" asked Pemberley once they had left Mrs Mullard's home.

"*Sneak* in, Pembers. Just like in *The Havana Heist*."

"But you said yourself that it would be both impossible and illegal!"

"I've changed my mind. I've had no choice but to change it, because I can't think of any other way to confirm the fact that Mr Lidcup is in possession of that recipe."

"But we could get ourselves arrested!"

"Only if we're found out. We'll just have to surround ourselves with experts."

"*Criminals*, you mean!"

"A locksmith isn't a criminal, Pembers. And while I'll freely admit that sneaking into the jam factory isn't completely lawful, there's no doubt that Lidcup's crimes are far worse. Just think of poor widowed Mrs Spooner! Hapless Mappin has no interest in helping her because Lidcup is a friend of his. It all leaves a very bitter taste in my mouth.

"Now, there'll be a lot to do over the next few days, so we'll need to divvy up the work. You go to Spooner's funeral and look out for any doctor's secretaries in attendance, and I'll meet with Mr Nightwalker. I presume he'll telephone us to confirm a meeting in the Pig and Scythe as soon as he sees the message in the newspaper tomorrow morning."

"That's what he usually does."

"Excellent. I've a good feeling about all this, Pembers. I think our efforts are really going to get us somewhere this time."

Chapter 23

SAWDUST COVERED the floor inside the Pig and Scythe public house and an odour of stale hops hung in the air. Carrying a tankard so as not to seem out of place, Churchill made her way over to a dingy corner of the room, where a man with a loosened tie and a shabby felt hat was napping at a table.

Churchill perched herself on a wooden stool across from him. "Mr Nightwalker?" she ventured.

He pushed up the brim of his hat to reveal a heavy brow and sharp blue eyes. "Ah, Mrs Churchill."

"Thank you for meeting with me."

"What do you need?"

"Where can I find someone who knows how to pick a lock?"

He glanced around the establishment. "I'd say most of the people in here could pick a lock."

"Can you recommend anyone in particular?"

He narrowed his eyes and surveyed the drinkers. "Mr Veltom."

"That name rings a bell. The number three bell at St Swithun's, to be precise."

"Yes, he's one of the bell-ringers. I hear they've all moved to South Bungerly now."

"That's because they fell out with Mr Spooner. I don't see why they can't move back to Compton Poppleford now, though."

"The ruddy great hole in the bell-ringing chamber floor might have something to do with it."

"Ah, yes. I suppose that'll need to be fixed first. Where is Mr Veltom?" Churchill recalled that he had curly hair and thick greying whiskers, but wasn't immediately able to spot him.

"He's over there, drinking with Malcolm Cogg."

"Another of the bell-ringers. Why would they choose to drink in this place?"

"What's wrong with it?"

"Nothing, if you like sawdust and dirty tankards."

"Do you want me to call him over?"

"In just a moment. First of all, have you ever come across this item, by any chance?" Churchill retrieved Pemberley's sketch of Mrs Higginbath's figurine from her handbag, unfolded it and handed it to Nightwalker.

"A naughty picture?"

"An eighteenth-century porcelain figurine of a courting couple. It was stolen a few weeks ago and I wondered if you'd come across anyone in here trying to sell it."

"The Wagon and Carrot's more your market for fancy figurines." He handed the sketch back to her.

"That's what I thought."

"It's usually the cheaper items that sell in here. Spades, boots…"

"Cattle prods."

"Cattle prods?"

"I'm only repeating what I've heard. Would you mind calling Mr Veltom over now?"

"I'll give him a nod."

The nod Nightwalker gave was too subtle for Churchill to notice. Mr Veltom quickly responded to it, however, and soon joined them at the table, tankard in hand.

"This is Mrs Churchill," said Nightwalker. "She's a detective."

"Aye."

"Have you met before?"

"Yeah, we've met," replied Mr Veltom. "You're lookin' for the person what dropped a bell on Spooner's 'ead. That's right, ain't it, Mrs Churchill?"

"Yes, that's right. It's nice to hear you speak at last, Mr Veltom. I recall that you were rather quiet at our last meeting."

"It's that Barnfather fella. I'm always nervous of sayin' the wrong thing in front of 'im. You've seen what 'e's like."

"I certainly have. He has a certain way about him."

"Barnfather's a bully," added Nightwalker.

"Is he? I can quite imagine that being the case now that you've mentioned it."

"Mrs Churchill has a job you might be interested in, Miles."

"What'll I be paid fer it?"

"Don't you want to hear what the job is first?" Nightwalker asked.

"I want to 'ear what I'll be gettin' paid first."

"Wait a minute," interrupted Churchill. "I need to know that I can trust you before we go any further. This job is top secret."

"Ain't they always?" replied Mr Veltom. "You can trust me, Mrs Churchill. Jus' the fact we're all sittin' at this table together shows we trust each other, don't it, Nightwalker?"

Nightwalker nodded.

"Oh, very well. How about a pound?" said Churchill.

"No, thanks. I ain't int'rested." Mr Veltom got up to leave.

"That's a shame," Churchill said. Then she turned to Nightwalker. "Didn't you say lots of people in here know how to pick locks?"

"Yes, quite a few of them. Maybe we can try someone else."

Mr Veltom paused. "Now, hold on, hold on." He sat down again. "I'm the best at pickin' locks around 'ere."

"But you're clearly too expensive for this task," responded Churchill. "If you're willing to walk away at a pound, there's not a lot more I can do."

"Maybe we can do a little negotiation." His dark eyes twinkled. "'Ow about three pound?"

"I'm sorry, Mr Veltom, but I really cannot stretch to three pounds. Thank you for your time. I shall have a chat with someone else in here."

"Now then, Mrs Churchill, I think you're being a little too 'asty. 'Ow about two pound an' five shillin's?"

"Still extremely overpriced, Mr Veltom. Thank you for the offer, though. It's been splendid talking to you."

He sighed. "Two pound?"

"One pound and five shillings."

"Done."

Mr Veltom spat into the palm of his hand and held it out to shake Mrs Churchill's. She donned a glove before shaking it in return.

"Now then, what's the job?" he asked.

"If I tell you, Mr Veltom, you must promise never to breathe a word of it to anyone."

"You have my word, Mrs Churchill."

"Excellent. We need to get inside the jam factory."

"The jam factory?" His eyes grew wide with interest. "We gonna steal some jam?"

"I'd rather not reveal the full plan just yet."

"Who else you got on the team?"

"Well, there's myself, my trusty assistant Miss Pemberley, our little dog Oswald, a former factory employee and you."

"We're gonna need more than that to get inside the jam factory."

"Yes, we are. I'm in the process of assembling a team."

He grinned. "I'm lookin' forward to it. I've never been in there meself. I'll need to know everythin' there is to know about the gates and doors, and all the different types o' locks."

"All in good time, Mr Veltom. Do you know of anyone who can break into a safe?"

"Break into a safe?" He laughed excitedly and rubbed his hands together with glee. "This sounds like a very interestin' job. As it 'appens, I know just the person!" He tapped the side of his nose.

"And who might that be?"

"Sally Tuffield. She fixes watches and used to be married to a watchmaker. She also 'appens to know a fair bit about gettin' inside safes."

"She sounds perfect. Where can I find her?"

"Down the little watch repairer's on the 'igh street. Next to the 'airdresser's, Curl Up and Dye. You ever been in there, Mrs Churchill?"

"Not that one, no. I go to La Coiffure."

"Very classy. Now, when you see Mrs Tuffield, tell 'er I send me warmest regards." He gave a little chuckle.

"Will she be pleased to receive them?"

"I dunno," he chuckled again. "You'll 'ave to let me know what she says! And if yer need any more suggestions from me, yer'll find me next door."

"You live next door to this public house, do you?"

"Yeah. Ain't a bad life, is it?"

Chapter 24

"Got a timepiece that wants fixing?" the watch repairer said without looking up.

Sitting at a high wooden desk, Mrs Tuffield was bent over a watch illuminated by a high-powered electric lamp. The walls of her little kiosk were covered with hooks, paper tags and watches waiting to be collected.

"Actually, no."

"No?"

She raised her head and Churchill started at the sight of the magnifying glass wedged into one of the watch repairer's eyes.

"Am I speaking with Mrs Tuffield?"

"Yes. What of it?" She had fair, curled hair, and her visible eye looked Churchill up and down. "You're the detective, aren't you?"

"Yes, that's right. Mrs Churchill."

"What can I do for you?" She returned to her work, her head bent over the watch again.

Churchill glanced around, checking that no one else

could have squeezed into the kiosk without her noticing. "I need some assistance with a little job, and I'm told you might be able to help me."

"Is that right?"

"Yes. Mr Veltom gave me your name."

"Did he now?"

"Are you able to help me, Mrs Tuffield?"

"Probably."

"Oh, good." Surprised by the watch repairer's nonchalance, Churchill decided to explain a little further just in case there was any room for misunderstanding. She lowered her voice. "We need to break into a safe."

Mrs Tuffield looked up again. "It's not a bank safe, is it? I don't do banks anymore. Too much work."

"No, not a bank safe. A jam factory safe."

"Lidcup's?"

Churchill looked around in panic, even though it would have been impossible for anyone to have joined them without her noticing. "Yes," she whispered. "But please don't breathe a word of it to anyone!"

Mrs Tuffield smiled, although the overall effect was disconcerting with the magnifying glass still wedged in her eye. "Folk like us don't usually go around talking, Mrs Churchill. You can trust me."

"Thank you." Churchill gave a sigh of relief, unaware of how nervous she had been feeling until that moment.

"Who else have you got?"

"Who else? My trusty assistant, a disgruntled former employee and Mr Veltom."

"If I know Miles, he'll be picking the locks. What about wheels?"

"Wheels?"

"You'll need to get us there and then away again. Fast!"

"Very true. I hadn't thought about wheels."

"You need to speak to Mrs Lillywhite. She's got a van. Uses it to take her husband's vegetables to the markets around and about, but she sometimes finds time for a spot of other work. She's down at Daisyview Farm."

"Has she done this sort of thing before?"

"Oh, lots of times. Her son's quite useful, too. A bit of muscle."

"Her son's a bit of muscle?"

"Yes. Large and pretty handy with his fists."

Churchill shuddered. "I really don't think we'll be needing any muscle."

Mrs Tuffield grinned. "I wouldn't pass him up, Mrs Churchill. You never know what might happen on a job like this."

Churchill felt a cold, uncomfortable sensation in her stomach as she walked back to the office. *Do I need someone who's handy with his fists?* she wondered. *Is it possible that a night-time heist at the jam factory could turn out to be very dangerous?* She couldn't imagine how. Perhaps Mrs Tuffield was thinking about bank raids, where people tended to arm themselves with weapons. *Surely there can be no real danger in sneaking into a jam factory and opening the safe.*

Churchill's discomfort worsened when she arrived at the office to find a visitor waiting for her.

"Mrs Higginbath," she said with a forced smile. "How lovely to see you."

"There's no need to lie, Mrs Churchill. Any sign of my figurine yet?"

"Has Miss Pemberley not filled you in?" She shot a

glance at her assistant, who was sitting at her desk, carefully stitching her prayer cushion cover.

"No. She told me to wait for you."

"I don't see why that was necessary. Miss Pemberley would have been more than capable of discussing the investigation with you." Churchill placed her hat on the hatstand and took a seat behind her desk. "Has she offered you some tea?"

"Yes. I've already drunk it."

"Good. How about cake?"

"I've already eaten it."

"Marvellous." Churchill peered hopefully into the cake tin on her desk and felt her heart sink further when she saw that it was empty.

"Well?" Mrs Higginbath stared unblinkingly at the disappointed detective.

"We've searched high and low for it. We even asked at the pawnbroker's shop and both public houses."

"Whatever for?"

"Those are the sorts of places a thief might try to sell a naughty ornament."

"A *naughty ornament*?"

"Sorry, that was a slip of the tongue. I meant to say an eighteenth-century porcelain figurine of a courting couple."

"I take it the thief hasn't tried to sell it, then?"

"No. He doesn't appear to have done."

"Then he's kept it for himself!"

"It's entirely possible."

"You'll have to go door to door looking for it, in that case."

"That's certainly one way of trying to find it."

"The only way, I'd say."

"Yes, although that would take up rather a lot of time. And there are only two of us."

"You need to recruit more staff, Mrs Churchill."

"That isn't my immediate plan, Mrs Higginbath. I don't have the necessary running costs for more staff at the present time."

Mrs Higginbath shrugged and stood to her feet. "I suppose I shall have to find somebody else if you're not up to the job."

"Not up to it? Of course I'm up to it!" Churchill also stood to her feet, trying to match Mrs Higginbath in height by standing on her tiptoes. "We've done a good job of eliminating the most obvious possibilities, and now we just need to—"

"Find it!"

"Absolutely."

"Right, well I'll leave you to it. I won't be holding my breath, Mrs Churchill. And to think that there was once the possibility of you receiving a library reading ticket for your trouble…" She gave a slow, disappointed shake of her head. "Never mind."

"That woman makes my blood boil!" snapped Churchill once Mrs Higginbath was out of earshot. "Why couldn't you have got rid of her before I returned, Pembers?"

"I didn't know how to."

"I've been dashing around, assembling a team for our heist, and the very last thing I needed was Mrs Higginbath here, making me feel weak and incapable."

"You're not weak or incapable, Mrs Churchill."

"Thank you, Pembers." Churchill sank back into her chair. "And with all the cake gone, I shall have to resort to eating the emergency eclair in my drawer."

She pulled it out and bit into it. In one swift moment, the smooth, sweet flavours of chocolate, pastry and cream banished her headache and warmed her insides. She looked down to see Oswald begging beside her chair.

"I can't believe you haven't taught this dog to leave people alone when they're eating yet, Pembers."

"Oh, I have. But people still give him titbits from time to time, so he just can't help himself."

"How was Mr Spooner's funeral?"

"It was a sombre affair. There weren't many people there."

"Any doctors' secretaries?"

"No. Miss Drumhead wasn't there, and I hadn't expected her to be. It's extremely unlikely that she would have had an affair with Mr Spooner."

"Any other potential lovers?"

"None that I could see. Mind you, how does one spot a potential lover?"

"Perhaps a heavily veiled lady standing on the periphery, quietly mourning alone?"

"I didn't see anyone like that. Did you give Oswald some of your chocolate eclair, Mrs Churchill?"

"No."

"Then why is he licking his lips?"

"A piece accidentally fell on the floor. And I stress the fact that it was very much accidental. I'm as disappointed to have missed out on it as he was happy to have found it. Was there anyone else at the funeral who looked at all mysterious?"

"No, although Mrs Thonnings was there. You don't think…?"

"That Mr Spooner's mistress could have been Mrs Thonnings? Oh golly, what a thought! She's probably the most likely candidate we can come up with at the present time, though she said that she didn't like him if I recall correctly."

"Perhaps that was just a ruse to put us off the scent."

"Perhaps it was. Oh dear. I'm not looking forward to asking her about it."

Chapter 25

Nestled in a nearby valley, Daisyview Farm was a short walk from Compton Poppleford. The farmhouse was painted a pleasing white, which glimmered in the sunshine as the two ladies and their dog walked along the rutted lane toward it. Neat rows of vegetables were growing in the fields either side of them.

"Farmer Lillywhite's well known for his cabbages," commented Pemberley. "I've heard he supplies the fancy guesthouses in Weymouth."

"Impressive. A lot of driving for Mrs Lillywhite, though. Is that their van I spy over there?"

Parked up next to the farmhouse, a small boy was polishing the shiny green vehicle. Yellow lettering on its side read: 'Lillywhite's Vegetables. A Vegetable for Every Table!'

Mrs Lillywhite was a warm, welcoming lady with a head of grey curls and a rosy complexion.

"You're in luck, ladies," she said, gesturing for them to

sit at the large wooden table in her kitchen. "I've just been doing a spot of baking."

"I've never felt so lucky," responded Churchill with a grin. Despite having barely exchanged more than a few words with Mrs Lillywhite, the portly detective had already decided she liked her.

"It's a pleasure to have you with us, Mrs Churchill and Miss Pemberley. I think it's wonderful that you've set yourselves up as private detectives."

"We certainly enjoy our work," responded Churchill as an enormous slice of strawberry sponge cake was placed in front of her.

"There's plenty more where that came from," said Mrs Lillywhite. "I baked four cakes this morning."

"Four?!"

"Oliver usually has one to himself, then we share out the rest."

"Oliver's your son, is he?" Churchill thought of the large fists and muscles Mrs Tuffield had previously mentioned.

"One of them. He's a big lad; needs a lot of feeding." She planted a large teapot at the centre of the table and sat down. "Now, how can I help you?"

"Mrs Tuffield mentioned your name. We're looking for someone with a vehicle."

"That would be me. Did you see my van parked outside?"

"We did."

"She's a good little runner, that one. Thirty brake horsepower, too."

"Excellent. I'm sure we can make good use of her if you're happy to help us. We have a small group of people who need transport to and from a local establishment after dark."

Mrs Lillywhite waggled her eyebrows excitedly. "Tell me more!"

"Well, I'd prefer not to give too much away just yet, as we need to keep everything under wraps. But I can tell you that the local establishment I mentioned is the jam factory."

"Lidcup's, eh? I've never been there myself, but a good number of my friends have been Lidcup Angels in the past. In fact, this sponge cake was made using Lidcup's jam!" She giggled. "Isn't that a funny coincidence?"

"It is, rather. Mrs Tuffield also mentioned that your son might prove useful."

"Oliver?"

"Is it true that he's good with his fists?"

"Extremely good." She leaned to one side and shouted at the top of her lungs: "Oliver!"

Oswald scrambled onto Pemberley's lap in terror.

"He'll be down in just a moment," said Mrs Lillywhite. "It always takes him a while to get moving. More cake?"

"Yes, please."

A little while later, the largest man Churchill had ever seen came lumbering into the kitchen. He gave the visitors a vacant look, then cracked his knuckles.

"This is Oliver," said Mrs Lillywhite, "my pride and joy. Would you like some cake, Oliver?"

The young man nodded and sat himself down in a sturdy-looking chair beside the iron stove. Mrs Lillywhite balanced two thick slices of cake on a plate and handed it to him.

"The trick is to never let him get hungry," she said as she returned to her seat. "We're all in trouble if Oliver gets hungry."

Churchill gave the young man an anxious look. "Shall

we bring supplies for him if he agrees to accompany us to the jam factory?"

"Leave the supplies to me, Mrs Churchill. I'll make sure he's provided for."

"I'm quite sure we won't need the use of his fists, but I suppose it'd be good to take him along just in case."

As the young man started cramming cake into his mouth, Churchill noticed that his hands were the size of snow shovels.

"He'll be extremely useful, especially when it comes to tackling the security guard," said Mrs Lillywhite.

Churchill felt a pang of alarm. "There's a security guard at the jam factory?"

"Aren't all factories guarded at night-time?"

"Yes, I suppose they are," replied Churchill weakly. Once again, she began to wonder whether she had taken on more than she could handle.

"I'm looking forward to it," said Mrs Lillywhite as she poured out the tea. "It'll make a nice change from delivering cabbages to Weymouth."

"Are you sure this jam factory heist is a good idea, Mrs Churchill?" Pemberley asked as the two ladies left the farm and headed back toward the village.

"I'd say that it's less of a good idea, Pembers, and more of my *only* idea."

"What happens if we get caught?"

"By whom?"

"Mr Lidcup, for one."

"That might not be such a bad thing if we can prove that he's in possession of the stolen jam recipe."

"And if he's not?"

"I'm sure we'll be able to talk ourselves out of it one way or another."

"I don't see how. We'll be committing a crime!"

"I realise that, but I don't see how else we can prove that Lidcup stole that recipe. Think of poor, grieving Mrs Spooner and how Mappin refuses to even consider Lidcup because the man happens to be one of his buddies! Disgraceful. In an unfair world we're forced to make decisions that place us within a grey area of the law, Pembers. And besides, we're to be accompanied by professionals! The likes of Mr Veltom, Mrs Tuffield and Mrs Lillywhite have done this sort of thing before. We're in safe hands."

"I'm not wholly convinced about that."

"I'm sure you'll begin to feel better about it after we've held our planning meeting."

"When will that be?"

"In the next day or two. In the meantime, shall we have a little word with Mrs Thonnings?"

"Good idea. I need to buy more prayer cushion supplies, anyway."

"How's the investigation going?" asked Mrs Thonnings a short while later as she crammed Pemberley's purchases into a striped paper bag.

"We have a suspect," answered Mrs Churchill.

"You do?" Her eyebrows shot up. "Who is it?"

"I'm afraid we're not at liberty to say at the moment, Mrs Thonnings, but rest assured that you shall find out soon enough. Did you enjoy Mr Spooner's funeral yesterday?"

"I don't think *enjoy* is quite the word."

"No, I should have used a different one," Churchill agreed.

"It was a nice send-off all the same."

"I expect you'll miss him."

The haberdasher shrugged. "It's always sad when someone dies, but I didn't know him very well."

"Did you not?"

"No. Miss Pemberley, I think it would be best if I used another bag for all these. The embroidery threads will get tangled if I squash them up much more."

"Are you sure you didn't know Mr Spooner very well?" probed Churchill.

"Quite sure. If I'd known him well I'd know it, wouldn't I? What an odd conversation this is turning out to be, Mrs Churchill."

"Are you aware that he had a special lady friend?"

"Really? Poor Mrs Spooner. She really has suffered."

"Do you happen to know who his lady friend might have been?"

"No. If I didn't know he had a lady friend, how could I possibly know who she was?"

"She may have attended his funeral."

"She may have done. There weren't many of us there, which isn't all that surprising. Very few people liked him."

"But you did."

"Not really, but he was always pleasant enough to me."

"Just pleasant? Or more than pleasant?"

"Are you implying something, Mrs Churchill?"

"Of course not."

"You have an odd look on your face and you're asking me all these strange questions. You're making me feel incredibly uneasy."

Mrs Churchill decided to mince her words no longer. "Were you his special lady friend, Mrs Thonnings?"

"No!" The haberdasher paused, embroidery threads in hand. "What sort of woman do you take me for?"

"Forget I asked it, Mrs Thonnings. It's just something I'm having to ask most of the ladies in the village because we really can't find out who it was."

"Did you ask Miss Pemberley?"

"No."

"Mrs Harris?"

"No."

"Mrs Higginbath?"

"No!"

"Then why me, Mrs Churchill? Why ask if *I* were his special lady friend?"

"Only because I know that you occasionally have special gentleman friends."

"Oh, I see. So when you hear that someone in the village has been having an extramarital affair, you immediately assume I'm the scarlet woman!"

"It really isn't like that at all, Mrs Thonnings."

The haberdasher sniffed. "Here are your bags, Miss Pemberley. I'm looking forward to seeing the prayer cushion when it's finished."

"Thank you, Mrs Thonnings," Pemberley replied.

"No, thank *you* for all your custom, Miss Pemberley. You make a haberdasher very happy."

"Typical," muttered Churchill after they had left the shop. "You're the one who makes Mrs Thonnings very happy and I'm the nasty one for upsetting her!"

"That's because you were the one who suggested she'd had an affair with Mr Spooner."

"*You* suggested it, Pembers. Don't you remember? You told me she was at the funeral, and that she must, therefore, have been his lover."

"Those weren't my exact words."

"Perhaps not. But if you hadn't suggested it in the first place, I wouldn't have gone and asked her about it and made her so upset!"

"Why don't you make a prayer cushion, too? She's bound to like you again if you spend a fortune in her shop."

"What an absolute nonsense of a suggestion, Pembers. Sometimes I feel as though I'm the one shouldering all the detective work while you swan about in my shadow with your dog."

"Well, it is your name on the door, Mrs Churchill."

"Should I add 'Pemberley' to it?"

"No, thank you."

Chapter 26

THE FOLLOWING EVENING, Churchill assembled her heist team in an upstairs room at the Wagon and Carrot. The sound of merrymaking rose up through the floorboards from the bar beneath and Churchill began to wish she had found Mrs Higginbath's figurine so they could have used the quiet library as a meeting place instead.

"I've brought paper and pencils," she said, placing them on the large table the crew was seated around. "Very important for planning! Does everybody here know each other?"

Mrs Mullard, Mr Veltom, Mrs Tuffield, Mrs Lillywhite and Oliver Lillywhite all gave each other a nod.

"Good. That makes things easier. Shall we begin? Let's start with you, Mrs Mullard. As a disgruntled former employee of Lidcup's, you're best placed to tell us about the inside workings of the factory. What time does it close?"

"Five o'clock is when the whistle goes. Then they're all out of there like rats down a drainpipe."

"Good. Is the place guarded at night?"

"Yes."

Churchill's heart sank. "Who guards it?"

"One-Eared Bob."

"He only has one ear?"

"I suppose he must have. Or must *haven't*."

"And is One-Eared Bob someone to worry about?"

"Well, you don't want him seeing you, because then he'll call the police."

"How can we distract him?" she asked the group.

Silence descended.

"What's the usual way to distract a security guard?" asked Churchill.

"Cosh 'im on the back of the 'ead," volunteered Mr Veltom.

"I see. Well, we won't be doing that to poor One-Eared Bob. Any other suggestions?"

"I could hide around the corner and make animal noises to distract him," suggested Mrs Lillywhite. "Then when he comes looking for me, you could all dash inside."

"Has that strategy ever been known to work before?"

"I've never tried it."

"What about a sleeping draught?" suggested Mrs Tuffield. She had a red circle around one eye where the magnifying glass usually sat.

"How would we administer it?" asked Churchill.

"In his food or drink," said Pemberley.

"And how would we do that?"

"I could make him a nice little cake and put a sleeping draught in it," said Mrs Lillywhite. "I'm not sure how I would give it to him, though."

"He has a security box by the front door," said Mrs Mullard. "You could leave it in there before he starts his shift with a note explaining that it's a gift. Knowing One-eared Bob, he'd fall for it, no problem."

"Excellent," said Churchill. "Once One-eared Bob is asleep, Mr Veltom can pick the lock on the front door."

"He'll need to pick the lock on the front gate first," said Mrs Mullard.

"Very well. Is that all right with you, Mr Veltom?"

"That's what I'm 'ere for!" He grinned, then winked at Mrs Tuffield. She responded with a scowl.

"And then Mr Veltom can pick the lock on the front door."

"He could try, but it wouldn't get him anywhere," commented Mrs Mullard.

"What d'yer mean it wouldn't get me nowhere?" retorted Mr Veltom. "I'm the best lock picker there is!"

"You may well be, but you still won't get anywhere because the front door is bolted from the inside."

"Oh dear," said Churchill. "Is there another door we can try?"

"The only way into the factory at night-time is through a short tunnel that leads into it from a trapdoor in the floor of One-Eared Bob's office."

"We have to go through the tunnel?"

"I wouldn't like to try it myself," said Mrs Mullard. "The trapdoor is right underneath One-Eared Bob's chair."

"Can't we just move his chair?"

"He'll be sitting in it, fast asleep."

"But what if he isn't?"

"Where else would he be if he was fast asleep?"

"Oh, I don't know. But surely it won't be a problem if we have to move his chair while he's in a deep sleep."

"We might accidentally knock him off it and then he'd wake up," said Pemberley.

"Or he might wake up anyway with all the jolting of being moved," said Mrs Lillywhite. "Too risky."

"There is an easier route," said Mrs Mullard.

"Which is?"

"Through one of the windows in the roof."

"For a moment there, I thought you said there was an *easier* route. The *roof*? How would we get onto the roof? I've seen how high it is and I certainly don't fancy climbing in through one of those windows!"

"You wouldn't have to, Mrs Churchill. All you need is someone who can climb up onto the roof, get through one of the windows, lower himself down and then slide back the bolt on the front door, allowing Mr Veltom to pick the lock and gain access."

"That sounds like an excellent plan," responded Churchill. "But which of us here would be willing to climb onto that roof?"

Another silence ensued.

Then Mr Veltom piped up. "I know just the man. And 'e's proberly downstairs in the bar at this very moment." He got up and left the room.

Churchill wiped her brow. This heist was proving more complicated than she had imagined. And yet, if it enabled her to find the stolen jam recipe in Mr Lidcup's safe, all the effort would have been worth it.

"While we're waiting for Mr Veltom to return, perhaps you could draw up a plan of the factory for us, Mrs Mullard," she suggested.

"Very well." The former factory employee picked up a pencil and began to sketch. "Right, then. This here's the gate, and this is One-eared Bob in his box."

"Does he stay in his box or does he walk around, patrolling the property?"

"I think he carries out regular patrols. Important to keep the legs moving, I suppose."

"But if he successfully consumes my little cake with the sleeping draught in it, he should remain in his box," said Mrs Lillywhite.

"Let's hope he does," said Churchill.

Mrs Mullard sketched some more. "The best way onto the roof is from this side of the building, where any of the windows in the roof can be accessed. This here is the main door, which can be unbolted by the person who gains access to the factory via the roof. You'll probably want to wait by that door so you can dash in as soon as it's open. Then you'll have to get right across the factory and over to the little office in the corner." She marked its location with an X. "The office has a locking door, so I expect Mr Veltom will need to pick that lock, too. Once you're inside the office, Mrs Tuffield can get to work on the safe."

Churchill turned to the watch repairer. "How long do you think it'll take you to crack the safe, Mrs Tuffield?"

"Anything between five minutes and five hours."

"*Five hours?* We can't possibly stay in the factory for that long!"

"What type of safe is it?"

"It's small and square with a dial and a handle on the front."

"Like I say, anything between five minutes and five hours."

"But hopefully on the quicker side rather than the slower side."

"Hopefully, yes. The big safes you get in banks tend to take a bit longer. I once spent a whole weekend inside a bank vault in Mayfair, but luckily no one noticed me and we cracked it in the end."

"Crikey!"

The door to the heist-planning room burst open.

"'Ere's yer man! None other than the number five bell-ringer!" announced Mr Veltom. "'E were in the bar downstairs, just like I thought!"

"Mr Whiplark?" exclaimed Churchill.

"Miss Churchley!"

The grey-bearded man was holding a tankard in his hand, and Churchill saw that Mr Veltom had also procured one for himself.

"Can we trust you?" Churchill asked the steeple keeper.

"I'm as trustworthy as the day is long!"

"Good. Then I suppose you'd better join us at the table. Just don't go slopping any scrumpy onto Mrs Mullard's drawing."

"Where've you got up to?" asked Mr Veltom.

"We were just talking about cracking the safe."

"Ooh, that's the excitin' part!"

"Exciting if it doesn't take too long, and we successfully break into it and find the stolen jam recipe."

"If I know Sally Tuffield, she'll be inside of that safe quick smart," said Mr Veltom, giving the watch repairer another wink. "And if you need an 'and, Sal, I know a little about safes meself."

"I won't need a hand," responded Mrs Tuffield stiffly.

"So waddya want me to do?" asked Mr Whiplark.

"Climb up onto the jam factory roof, gain access through one of the windows, lower yourself down and then slide open the bolt on the main door so we can get in," replied Churchill.

"That should be easy-peasy."

"Do you have ladders and ropes?"

"I'm a steeple keeper. Course I got ladders and ropes!"

"How will we transport the ladders?" asked Pemberley.

"On the roof of Mrs Lillywhite's van, I suppose," replied Churchill. "Would we be able to strap a ladder to your van's roof?" she asked the farmer's wife.

"Shouldn't be a problem."

"Excellent."

"Who's going to act as lookout?" asked Mrs Lillywhite.

"That's a very good question indeed," said Churchill. "How many lookouts do you think we'll need?"

"I'd say two, just in case something happens to one of them."

"What's likely to happen to one of them?"

"I don't know. They could fall asleep or have an episode of some sort… a medical episode, perhaps, or maybe the police will find and arrest them. You should always have at least two lookouts, Mrs Churchill."

"Fine. How about you, Mrs Mullard? Do you fancy being one of our lookouts?"

"All right."

"She can observe the main entrance," said Mrs Lillywhite. "She needs to keep a close eye on it to make sure nobody else goes in there."

Churchill gave this some thought. "And supposing Mrs Mullard does spot somebody going in through the main entrance. How will she alert those who are inside the factory?"

"She could flash a light at one of the high windows so it can be seen from the other side of the factory wall."

"How would we get access to such a window?"

"There's a few premises overlookin' the factory," said Mr Veltom. "Maybe she could sit by the window in one o' them to get a good angle."

"Good idea," said Churchill. "Does anybody know of someone who owns or rents one of those properties?"

"Mr 'Oskins the 'ardware shop owner's a good friend o' mine," said Mr Whiplark. "I could ask 'im."

"His property overlooks the factory entrance, does it?"

"Yeah, it's right opposite."

"Tremendous. One other troubling matter comes to mind, however. How do you intend to ask Mr Hoskins about accessing his property without telling him the plan?"

"Oh, me and 'Oskins goes back a long way. 'E knows not to ask too many questions."

"How will we see Mrs Mullard's flashing light if we're inside the factory?" asked Pemberley.

"A very good point," replied Churchill.

"I'll park in the street, where I can watch the window," said Mrs Lillywhite. "If I see the light flashing, I'll parp the horn."

"Perfect!" said Churchill. "If we hear the parps we'll know to get out of there swiftly." She rubbed her brow. "There's a lot that could go wrong here, but all in all I think we have a decent plan. Does anyone have anything else to add?" She addressed the young man seated beside his mother. "You've been rather quiet, Oliver. Do you have any questions or suggestions?"

The large young man shrugged.

"That means he's happy," said Mrs Lillywhite.

"Brilliant!"

"What will my role be?" asked Pemberley.

"In addition to the very important job of being my aide-de-camp, Miss Pemberley, you can be responsible for timings. Keep an eye on the watch. We need everything to run like clockwork, and I think you're the perfect woman for the job."

"But I don't have a watch."

"I can lend you one," said Mrs Tuffield. "And a stop-watch, too."

"Wonderful," said Churchill. "That just about covers everything, I think. Save for a few minor details, I think we're finally ready to put our plan into action!"

Chapter 27

"I'M SO NERVOUS," said Pemberley as the two ladies mentally prepared for the break-in over afternoon tea at the tea rooms. "What if something goes wrong?"

"There's always something that could go wrong, Pembers. The important thing is how we react to it."

"And how should we react to it?"

"It depends on what it is that goes wrong."

"That's exactly why I'm so nervous! It's dealing with the unknown."

"We have an excellent plan. Surely that should make it all seem a little less unknown. If we stick to the plan, all will be well. You've made a note of all the timings, haven't you?"

"Yes. Mrs Lillywhite puts the cake laced with sleeping draught in One-Eared Bob's box at five o'clock before he comes on shift at six o'clock. Then just before ten o'clock she begins her round, collecting us all up. She starts with Mrs Tuffield at ten, followed by Mrs Mullard at three minutes after ten—"

"There's no need to recite all the timings now, Pembers. As long as you know exactly what's happening and when, we shall be fine."

"All right."

"Why are you making that odd breathing sound?"

"I'm trying to calm my nerves."

"You're overthinking it all. Just pretend, for a moment, that our little sojourn this evening isn't happening at all. Pretend you'll just be having an ordinary evening at home."

"How I wish I was!"

"Let's pretend that you are, then."

"All right."

"Forget all about our plan to retrieve the stolen jam recipe."

"Oh, now you've gone and reminded me! I'd forgotten all about it for a moment."

"It's good that you were able to forget about it for a moment, Pembers. Try doing the same thing again."

"All right."

"You don't need to make that strange breathing noise, though. People are beginning to look over at our table."

"Deep breathing calms me down."

"Try to do it a little more quietly, then."

In truth, Churchill was feeling just as nervous as her assistant. Having to calm Pemberley down served as a good distraction from her own nerves, however. She hummed a tuneless ditty as she buttered her scone, keen to demonstrate that any thought of the evening's heist was no bother to her at all. She reached for the little pot of jam. "It's funny, isn't it, when you see the Lidcup's label on the jam jar." She chuckled.

"You've just reminded me again of what's happening

this evening, Mrs Churchill! I'd managed to forget for about half a minute!"

"Oh dear, I am sorry." As Churchill spooned out the jam, she decided to give up on trying to calm her assistant's nerves. The sooner the evening was over and done with, the better.

Chapter 28

CHURCHILL STOOD and watched the lane from her cottage window at a quarter past ten that evening with the lights off.

A flash of headlights appeared at exactly the appointed time. Grabbing her handbag, she scurried out of her cottage and crept noiselessly up to Mrs Lillywhite's van. Wary of using a torch, Churchill relied on her hearing to guide her.

The van door creaked open, then she heard a whisper. "It's quite a step up, Mrs Churchill. Mind how you go."

"Where are you?"

There was no sign of Mrs Lillywhite in the dark lane.

"Behind you."

"What? How did you get there?"

"Don't worry about that now. Just hop in. We've a schedule to keep."

"Yes, we have."

Hands stretched out in front of her, Churchill felt her way to the back of the van. The floor was higher than she had anticipated and she scraped her knee as she clambered in. There was very little room inside. Wherever her hands went, they came into contact with a moving form.

"Good evenin', Mrs Churchill," came Mr Veltom's voice.

She swiftly let go of the leg she had just clasped.

"Can you budge up?" she hissed.

"We've already budged up!"

"Is everyone in?" asked Mrs Lillywhite from behind Churchill.

"I assume so, although it's a little too dark to tell."

The door slammed shut and the engine started up a moment later.

"Prepare yourself, Mrs Churchill," said Pemberley's voice. "She drives quite—"

Before Pemberley could finish her sentence, the engine revved and the van tore off down the bumpy lane, forcing Churchill back against the rear doors. For once, she was pleased it was dark because she felt sure her petticoat was on display.

"Oof!" She briefly managed to rearrange herself, but then the van took a sharp corner to the right. She tumbled into the lap of someone who turned out to be Mr Veltom again.

"Good evenin', Mrs Churchill. We must stop bumpin' into one another like this."

She did her best to regroup and drag herself over to the opposite side of the van.

"Who's that?" said Mrs Tuffield's voice.

"Me," she puffed. "Mrs Churchill."

"There's no room on this side."

The van took another sharp turn and Churchill tumbled over again.

"Good grief!" she exclaimed. "Who's got their head beneath my knees?"

When no reply came, she did her best to move her knees away from the head before reaching her hand down to give the person a gentle nudge.

She hadn't expected to feel rough, dry skin against the smooth skin of her hand. "Ugh!" she said, recoiling. "Who's that?"

"What is it, Mrs Churchill?" asked Pemberley.

"Who's got strange skin on their head?" A shiver ran up her spine. "It's all rough and bumpy! It's—"

"A cabbage," replied Pemberley. "I had a similar fright myself when I got in, Mrs Churchill. There are several rolling around with us. Mrs Lillywhite apologised about it earlier. They're just today's rejects from Weymouth."

"A cabbage? Oh, thank goodness for that. Are we nearly there yet?"

"I hope so."

The van began to jolt violently up and down, and Churchill could only surmise that they were bouncing along the cobbled high street. She pictured the inevitable bruising on her posterior and hoped the vigorous shaking of her brain would have no lasting effects.

"I could have sworn the high street was only about half as long as this," she moaned as the jolting went on and on. "A third of it, perhaps! Where are we? Are we even on the high street?" Just as Churchill was beginning to wonder whether she was destined to spend the rest of her days being interminably thrown about in complete darkness, the van wheels reached a smoother surface.

"Thank heavens!"

She felt a gentle nudge at her elbow, followed by the unmistakeable sensation of a tongue against her cheek.

"Mr Veltom!" she roared. "If that's you, I'll—"

"What?" came his voice from the other side of the van.

"Who's licking me?"

"That'll be Oswald," said Pemberley. "He always licks people when he's nervous."

"Oh, Oswald." Churchill reached out and cuddled the warm little dog. "Thank goodness you're here. We can endure this ordeal together." She closed her eyes and allowed the little dog to lick her face some more.

"Almost there!" came Mrs Lillywhite's distant voice from the front of the van.

"Oh, thank goodness, thank goodness..." began Churchill, but the momentary calm was interrupted by a sharp lurch to the right, soon followed by a swerve to the left.

Oswald leapt away from Churchill and the van lurched to a sudden halt, sending her rolling back against the rear doors once again.

"Oh, golly," she said with a sigh. "What a ride! And now there's another of those pesky cabbages in my lap."

"Not a cabbage this time, Mrs Churchill," Mr Veltom's voice announced. "It's me 'ead!"

Chapter 29

The bedraggled team clambered out of the van and found themselves standing in front of the tall, shadowy factory gates.

Pemberley shone a torch onto her watch. "We're bang on time," she confirmed.

"Excellent!" whispered Churchill. "Mr Veltom?"

"Here."

"Time to do your work."

His shadowy form shuffled forward and Churchill held her breath as she listened to the faint tinkering noise of a lock being picked.

Behind them, Mrs Lillywhite and Mr Whiplark were busy untethering the ladder from the roof of the van. Churchill was amazed it had remained in place during the van's tempestuous journey.

"All done," came Mr Veltom's whisper.

Churchill heard a creak as the factory gate began to swing open.

"Just push it open a little bit," she whispered. "We don't want it opening all the way."

The van drove off and parked beside the hardware store a short distance away. Mrs Mullard was to keep lookout from the window above the store.

Churchill counted each member of the group as they carefully squeezed through the half-open gate. Once they were through, Mr Veltom closed it again and the dark outline of the factory loomed ahead of them. The factory yard was dark and the cobbles beneath Churchill's feet felt uneven. A dim light glimmered from a little window, which Churchill guessed was One-Eared Bob's box.

"We need to make sure the security guard's asleep," she said. "Who'd like to creep up there and find out?"

"I'll go," said Mrs Lillywhite.

They waited patiently as the dark form of the farmer's wife slipped away.

"She's been gone one minute so far," said Pemberley after a short while.

"Thank you, Miss Pemberley."

They waited in silence a little while longer.

"How long has she been gone now, Miss Pemberley?"

"One minute and forty seconds."

Churchill felt her heart thud with impatience. Even though it was pitch black, she still worried someone might somehow spot them there.

"He's asleep!" came the welcome whisper from Mrs Lillywhite.

"Thank goodness for that," whispered Churchill in reply. "And well done with your cake plan. Right then, let's get over to the shadows by the wall so Mr Whiplark can do his bit. Where's Oswald?"

"I've got him on a lead," replied Pemberley. "I didn't want him running off in the dark."

"Exceptionally sensible, Pembers. Let's go, everyone;

quietly as you can. Are you all right with your ladder, Mr Whiplark?"

"Fine 'n' dandy. Miles is 'elpin' me carry it."

The group crept silently over the cobbles toward the dark outer wall of the factory. It wasn't long before they reached the large doors at the main entrance.

"Right. I'll get up onto that roof," said Mr Whiplark.

"Have you got your ropes?"

"Wrapped round me shoulder."

"Excellent. Good luck, Mr Whiplark. We'll see you shortly."

Mr Veltom helped place the ladder against the factory wall, then held it as the steeple keeper clambered up. Churchill glanced back nervously at the security guard's box, worried he might suddenly awaken. Fortunately, all was quiet. She remained aware of the large, silent form of Oliver Lillywhite close by, just in case any trouble arose.

Mr Veltom let go of the ladder and Mr Whiplark disappeared into the darkness.

"Well, that's 'im gone," Mr Veltom said matter-of-factly.

"Rather him than me," said Mrs Tuffield. "I can't stand heights."

"How long did we give Mr Whiplark for his part, Miss Pemberley?" asked Churchill.

"We worked out that he has a total of six minutes."

"Good." Churchill leaned back against the rough bricks of the factory wall, aware that the next six minutes was likely to feel more like six hours.

"I s'pose we just 'ave to stand 'ere and entertain ourselves fer now," said Mr Veltom.

"There's no need for entertainment right now," said Churchill. "We must wait patiently. The time will soon pass."

"Sally Tuffield's got a few party tricks. Ain't that right, Sal?"

"Not anymore, Miles," she replied dryly.

"Not anymore? I don't believe it. You're just pretendin' 'cause we're in polite comp'ny. What's that joke yer used ter tell? The one about the nurse and the bank manager."

"I think you're getting me mixed up with Mrs Thonnings."

"Nah. I'm sure it were you, Sal."

"It certainly wasn't."

"Yeah, it was."

Churchill felt a snap of impatience. "How much longer, Miss Pemberley?"

"Four minutes."

"I often think about them good old days, Sal," continued Mr Veltom. "Don't you never dwell on 'em yerself?"

"I can't say that I do."

"Breaks a man's 'eart to 'ear that, it does."

"I'm sure you'll survive, Mr Veltom," said Churchill.

"Oh, he will," added Mrs Tuffield.

"I won't. I'm lovelorn." He hummed the first line of a ditty about a broken heart.

"Oh, no, Mr Veltom," said Churchill. "Please stop."

To her dismay, he started singing instead; quietly at first, but then the pitch began to rise.

"Mr Veltom!" she snapped.

The fierce tone of her voice silenced him.

"Thank goodness for that!" said Pemberley.

"How much longer?" asked Churchill.

"Three minutes."

"I dunno 'ow we're supposed ter pass the time if I ain't allowed ter sing," said Mr Veltom sullenly.

"It'll pass more quickly if you just keep quiet," replied Mrs Tuffield.

"Oh, Sal! I can just about cope with Mrs Churchill tellin' me off, but you? I can't bear it!"

"Let's play a little game of *I Spy*," said Churchill, desperate to drown out Mr Veltom's voice.

"Oh, me first!" responded Mr Veltom. "I spy with my lil eye, somethin' beginnin' with 'F'."

"Factory," said Pemberley.

"I knew you'd say that! But that ain't it."

Churchill glanced around, her view of any surrounding objects severely limited by the dark. "It has to be 'factory', Mr Veltom. What else could possibly begin with 'F' around here?"

He cackled. "You're gonna 'ave to keep guessin'!"

"Frock?" suggested Mrs Tuffield.

"That's a good one, Sal, but no."

"What else could it possibly be?"

"Keep guessin'."

"Fox?"

"Where's a fox?" he queried.

"There might be one near here."

"It ain't fox."

"Foot?"

"Nope."

"Feet?"

"Nope."

"It could be feet. We've all got them," Mrs Tuffield reasoned.

"It could be factory, 'n' all, but it ain't."

"That's six minutes," said Pemberley. "Mr Whiplark should be pulling back the bolt on that door any moment now."

"Thank heavens." Churchill edged closer to the door.

"Fog?" said Mrs Tuffield.

"It ain't foggy, Sal!" laughed Mr Veltom.

"Food?"

Churchill ignored a sudden rumble in her stomach. "Where can Mr Whiplark be?" she asked.

"Forget-me-not," said Mrs Tuffield.

"Me favourite flower, Sal! D'yer remember?"

"Where's Mr Whiplark, Pembers?" interjected Churchill.

"I don't know. I'm getting a little worried."

"Is it possible that we misjudged the timings?"

"We spent a lot of time working them out," replied Pemberley. "I can't imagine them being enormously off. He's a whole two minutes late! What could have happened to him?"

"Let's give him ten minutes," suggested Mrs Tuffield.

"Then what?" asked Mr Veltom.

"We switch to another plan."

"What other plan?"

"I'm sure Mrs Churchill has one."

"Another plan?" said Churchill. "Erm… Do we have another plan, Miss Pemberley?"

"I don't know. Do we?"

"That's what I asked you." Despite the darkness, Churchill felt all eyes on her. The least she could do was try to reassure them. "Oh, the *other plan*. Yes, we can switch to the other plan if needs be."

"What is the other plan?" asked Mr Veltom.

"I'll tell you if it becomes apparent that Mr Whiplark has been unable to open the door for some reason."

There was an uneasy silence for a few moments, then Pemberley switched on her torch and checked her watch. "It's been ten minutes now."

Churchill pressed her ear against the main door,

praying she would hear the bolt slide across at any moment. It was worryingly silent.

"Right then," she said, her breath a little shaky. "Time for the other plan. Follow me." She switched on her torch and began to lead her team off to the right-hand side of the factory building. She'd swiftly decided that her alternative plan would be to find another way inside. It seemed unlikely, but she had no idea what else to do.

As they reached the first corner, Churchill paused and turned around. "Is everybody with me?" she whispered. "Miss Pemberley and Oswald? Mr Veltom? Mrs Tuffield? Oliver Lillywhite?"

"All here," replied Mr Veltom.

Oliver Lillywhite grunted and Churchill realised this was the first sound she had ever heard from him.

"What's the other plan, Mrs Churchill?" asked Pemberley.

"Well, we now have two objectives. The first is to get inside the safe to retrieve the stolen jam recipe and the second is to locate Mr Whiplark."

"I wonder what's happened to him," commented Mrs Tuffield.

"Proberly fell off the roof," said Mr Veltom.

"Oh, don't!" responded Mrs Tuffield. "The thought of even the smallest of heights makes me feel giddy."

"I'm sure there's a logical explanation," said Churchill. "There always is. Now, we need to sidle along this next wall and look for another way in."

Mr Veltom gave a low guffaw. "We'll be lucky. Everything's bolted and the only access is via an underground tunnel beneath One-Eared Bob."

"We must hold out hope."

"Is that all we're relyin' on now? 'Ope?"

"I'm afraid so."

"I think it's a very sensible plan, Mrs Churchill," said Mrs Tuffield.

"Why, thank you."

"Me too," added Pemberley.

"Good. Let's keep going." Churchill marched on, following the beam of her torch with the factory wall on her left-hand side.

Her hopes rose when she came across a blue metal door. She stopped to examine it. "I can't see a lock," she whispered, "or even a handle. It looks like the sort of door that can only be opened from the inside."

"Not much use to us, then," said Mrs Tuffield. "Onwards?"

"Yes. On we go."

As she walked, Churchill wondered what would happen if they walked around the entire perimeter of the factory without finding another way in. Any hope of retrieving the stolen recipe would have to be abandoned. *But what of Mr Whiplark?* she mused. *It wouldn't be fair to leave him to his unhappy plight. What if he's plummeted through a window?*

Churchill tried to push away any thought of the steeple keeper lying injured on the factory floor. She felt responsible for his welfare.

"I don't wanna alarm no one," came Mr Veltom's voice from behind her. "But I think I jus' saw a light."

Churchill stopped. "What sort of light?"

"A torchlight."

"*My* torchlight?"

"No, not *yours*, Mrs Churchill. I ain't *that* stupid. There's someone behind us."

"Where behind us?" Churchill turned off her torch and peered beyond the dark figures behind her.

Mr Veltom wasn't mistaken.

There was a faint light in the distance.

And it was moving!

Churchill's mouth felt dry. "Perhaps it's Mr Whiplark," she stammered.

"Could be," replied Mr Veltom. "But I reckon it's more likely that old One-Eared Bob's woke up."

Chapter 30

"One-eared Bob's woken up?" exclaimed Churchill. "But what about the sleeping draught in his cake?"

"Mebbe it didn't work," replied Mr Veltom.

"Oh, heavens!"

"He's going to see us!" hissed Pemberley.

"Not if we can get inside this building right away."

"We need to stop the plan! We need to abandon ship!"

"And leave Mr Whiplark stranded?"

"What else can we do? He's got himself into trouble somehow, and now the security guard is on the prowl. This is a complete disaster!"

"It isn't, Pembers," replied Churchill. "We can still find a way in."

"Yes, we can," replied Mrs Tuffield. "It's not clear whether One-Eared Bob has actually spotted us or whether he's just doing one of his regular patrols. But either way, we can't hang about here waiting to find out. We need to move!"

"That's the spirit, Sal," agreed Mr Veltom. "Let's go!"

Churchill turned her torch on again and broke into a

jog, breathing in great mouthfuls of evening air. Her mind swung between panic and calm. *Will we be caught? No, everything will be all right. But what if we are?*

"A door!" hissed Pemberley.

They all stopped suddenly.

"No handle or lock again," commented Churchill. "But there is a little window."

"Maybe too little," commented Mrs Tuffield. "Only a very thin person could climb through that."

Churchill examined it. "It's jammed shut."

"Shouldn't be a problem," said Mr Veltom.

He stepped forward, took a small tool out of his pocket and began working at the window frame. "Can you shine your torch on it, Mrs Churchill? I can't work on this sort of thing in the dark."

Churchill did so and anxiously glanced behind her again. Her heart gave a heavy thud. "Oh, cripes! He's getting closer! Hurry up, Mr Veltom."

A moment later, he pulled the window open. "There yer go. Who's goin' in?"

"Excellent work, Mr Veltom! Come along, then, Miss Pemberley. In you go."

"Climb through the window? But why me?"

"You're the only person who's slender enough. And One-eared Bob is bearing down on us fast! Please, Miss Pemberley!"

"And I'm to open the door from the other side?"

"Yes, yes! In you go!"

"Oh, very well. Who's going to hold Oswald for me?"

"I will," said Mrs Tuffield. "And Oliver will lift you in."

"Really? But I'm not as light as I look. Woah!"

Before she could say another word, Pemberley was lifted off her feet and Oliver had begun inserting her through the open window, headfirst.

"All right!" she hissed. "I've got this now. You can let go of me and I'll rest on the windowsill."

The boy did as he was told and Churchill watched as Pemberley disappeared through the window.

"Good luck, Pembers!" she whispered after her.

She turned off her torch, hoping the sudden absence of light would cause the security guard to lose interest. It was a vain hope, however. As she listened to Pemberley scrabbling with the latch on the other side of the door, One-Eared Bob's torch grew closer still.

"Someone's gonna 'ave to deal with 'im," said Mr Veltom ominously.

"Maybe not," replied Churchill. "Maybe we can get inside just in time and shut the door on him."

"But he'll know we're in there!"

"Oh, do hurry up, Pembers!"

There was a click of a latch and a thud, then the door swung open with a loud creak.

"Oh, thank goodness!"

"Oi!" came a shout from behind them.

"Quick! Get inside!"

"Oliver, detain him!" ordered Mrs Tuffield.

"But don't hurt him," pleaded Churchill. "Just detain him." She dashed in through the dark doorway, swiftly followed by Mr Veltom and Mrs Tuffield, still carrying Oswald. Pemberley pulled it closed and Churchill switched on her torch.

There was a muffled cry beyond the door and Churchill prayed that One-Eared Bob wouldn't be injured in any way.

"It's safe to say that we've been discovered," she said sadly. "All we can do now is retrieve Mr Whiplark and the jam recipe as quickly as possible."

The beam of her torch glinted off hundreds of glass

jars as she flashed it around the room. "We're in the bottling section," she said. "We need to get over to Mr Lidcup's office. You can pick the lock, Mr Veltom, then Mrs Tuffield can start work on the safe. While you're doing that, Miss Pemberley and I will search for Mr Whiplark."

"Sounds like a plan," said Mr Veltom.

They scurried across the factory floor, which felt slightly sticky beneath Churchill's feet. Oswald trotted alongside them.

"There you are!" echoed a voice far above their heads.

Churchill halted and shone her torch upwards.

"Over 'ere, Miss Churchley!"

Her torch beam came to rest on Mr Whiplark, who was dangling from the end of a rope about fifteen feet above their heads. She gasped. If he were to fall from such a height, he could break a leg or even his neck. It didn't bear thinking about.

"Golly, Mr Whiplark! Are you stuck?"

"Yeah. Me rope weren't long enough. Roof was 'igher than I thought. Sorry about that."

"How on earth are we going to get you down from there?"

"I ain't got no idea. I've jus' been swinging about in the 'opes I could reach one o' them pillars. But I've worn meself out."

"I expect you have. We'll try to help, but we're running rather short on time. One-Eared Bob is already on to us and is currently being detained by Oliver outside."

"Go on an' get the safe open," he replied. "I'll try swingin' again."

Churchill turned to Mrs Tuffield and Mr Veltom. "I'll show you where the office is." Then she turned to Pemberley. "Have a look around and see if you can find something long and thin that you can poke up to Mr Whiplark to get him swinging again. Hopefully he can grab hold of one of those pillars and somehow get himself down from there."

Churchill led the way to the office and they climbed the steps. Mr Veltom picked the lock in no time.

They stepped inside and Churchill turned on a desk lamp. "Here's the safe, Mrs Tuffield. What do you think?"

"Looks straightforward enough," she replied with a nod.

"Oh, that's wonderful news. We're almost there."

As Mrs Tuffield pulled a pouch of tools from her jacket and crouched down in front of the safe, Churchill allowed herself a glimmer of optimism. Could their mission almost be complete?

"We'll leave you to it, Mrs Tuffield. Mr Veltom and I will go back and see what we can do to get Mr Whiplark down from the ceiling."

Churchill and Mr Veltom returned to the main factory floor. There was no sign of Pemberley or Oswald, and Mr Whiplark was beginning to look rather floppy.

"That don't look good," commented Mr Veltom. "'Ow you doin' up there, Brian?"

"To be honest with yer, Miles, I've been puttin' a bit of a brave face on it. Despite me best efforts, me 'ead keeps sinkin' down lower than the rest o' me body. I don't think I'm gonna last too much longer up 'ere."

"Oh, golly," said Churchill. "Where's Pemberley got to?"

"I'm over here," she replied, emerging from the shadows with a torch in one hand and a long wooden pole in the other. She positioned herself beneath Mr Whiplark and held the pole up above her head. "Here you go. Grab hold of this."

At least five feet remained between the end of the pole and Mr Whiplark. He made a feeble attempt to reach down, presumably just to show willing. But it was no use; the pole was no help at all.

"What we need is another rope," said Churchill. "If we had another rope we could throw it up to Mr Whiplark and we could swing him over to a pillar."

"That's a good idea," said Mr Whiplark.

"Righty-'o," said Mr Veltom. "Let's look for one."

Churchill anxiously flashed her torch in the direction of the manager's office to see whether there was any sign of Mrs Tuffield having broken into the safe. All she could see was the dim light through the window. There had been no success just yet.

Churchill, Pemberley and Mr Veltom scurried around the various parts of the factory flashing their torches onto shelves and into cupboards, desperately searching for a rope. Oswald scampered after Pemberley, giving little excited barks as his mistress dashed here and there.

"Oh, heck," Churchill muttered to herself. "Sooner or later, One-Eared Bob's going to raise the alarm. Each minute spent here brings us closer to being found out." She pulled open a cupboard, which was filled with bags of sugar. There was no rope to be seen anywhere. "This was a stupid idea," she continued, "I've been such a fool! I've taken on too much, as always. Now we're going to end up in big trouble. We're going to get caught."

Then she heard the murmur of excitement, followed by her name being called. She dashed back to the main factory floor, shone her torch toward the office and saw Mrs Tuffield's head poking out through the door.

"All open, Mrs Churchill!"

A wave of relief flooded over her.

Forgetting all about the rope and Mr Whiplark for a moment, she dashed over to the office and thundered up the little steps as fast as her legs would carry her. Huffing and puffing, she practically fell into the office, where the safe door stood joyously wide open.

"Well done, Mrs Tuffield! You're very clever! Thank you so much."

Churchill sank to her knees in front of the safe and shone her torch inside it. As expected, there were a number of dog-eared, sticky jam recipes within. She pulled them out and, sure enough, found a hand-scrawled recipe entitled 'Secret Spooner Family Recipe for Plum Jam'.

"This has to be it!" she exclaimed. "He did steal it after all!"

"There are some other interesting items in here, too," commented Mrs Tuffield, shining her own torch inside the safe. "Some jewellery… and a few ornaments. Plus a number of envelopes stuffed full of banknotes. How interesting."

Churchill peered inside again. "It's a little treasure trove! And if I'm not mistaken, one of those ornaments looks very much like an eighteenth-century porcelain figurine of a courting couple. It's Mrs Higginbath's naughty ornament!"

The happy sensation brought on by this discovery was immediately interrupted by the distant parp of a horn.

Churchill started. "Oh, golly! Could that be Mrs Lillywhite's van?"

Mrs Tuffield responded to Churchill with a nervous glance. "I fear it was. We need to get out of here right away!"

"I'll take the recipe and figurine so we can return them to their rightful owners," said Churchill, hurriedly shoving them into her handbag and closing the safe door. She stood to her feet. "And we still need to get poor Mr Whiplark down from the ceiling."

Churchill and Mrs Tuffield rushed out of the office to

find Pemberley and Mr Veltom attempting to throw a rope up to Mr Whiplark.

"Oh, you found one!" said Churchill.

The steeple keeper, however, was beginning to look rather feeble, and his attempts to grab the rope were increasingly weak.

"It's no good," said Pemberley. "We can't always get the rope up high enough, and even when we do, he isn't able to grab hold of it."

"We need to get out of here," said Churchill, her heart thudding furiously. "We've just heard Mrs Lillywhite's horn parping."

"Just go!" Mr Whiplark called down. "Lidcup'll call the fire brigade when he finds me 'ere. They'll get me down."

"But you'll be in terrible trouble, Mr Whiplark!" said Churchill.

At that moment, Mr Whiplark managed to catch the rope Mr Veltom had been repeatedly throwing up to him.

"Well done, Brian!"

Mr Whiplark clung on to the rope as tightly as his remaining strength allowed. "Yer'll 'ave ter swing me over to a pillar," he called down.

"I'll try." Mr Veltom began frantically running to and fro, and before long he managed to get Mr Whiplark swinging again.

The old man at the end of the rope began to groan.

"What's the matter?" Churchill called up to him.

"I'm feelin' seasick!"

"You'll be fine, Brian," said Mr Veltom. "We'll soon 'ave yer down from there. He began to run even faster, then suddenly gave a loud grunt and crumpled to the floor.

"Oh, good grief!" Pemberley cried out. "What's happened?"

Mr Veltom lay on the floor, groaning almost as loudly as Mr Whiplark. "I tripped! That's me ankle gone now."

Suddenly, the factory was illuminated with a blast of light.

"Oh, good heavens!" exclaimed Churchill. "We're done for!"

Chapter 31

"I DON'T EVEN KNOW where to start," said Inspector Mappin. He opened his notebook and swiftly closed it again. Then he scratched his head. "I really don't know where to start," he added.

He stood at the centre of the factory floor wearing a cosy pullover, flannel slacks and slippers. Having been called out at such a late hour, he clearly hadn't found the time to change into his uniform. Beside him stood a scowling Mr Lidcup. His oiled, wavy hair was a little dishevelled, and the distinctive odour of brandy and cigars was emanating from him.

Close by, two firemen were folding up their ladder, having rescued the unfortunate Mr Whiplark from the ceiling of the factory. He was lying on the floor close by, being tended to by Mrs Tuffield. Mr Veltom was lying close by in a bid to entice Mrs Tuffield to tend to him in like manner.

A tall, hatchet-faced man with one ear surveyed the intruders contemptuously, his arms folded over a torn and dirty blue uniform. The large form of Oliver Lillywhite loomed beside him, one eye slightly bruised.

"Mrs Churchill," began Inspector Mappin for the second time. "What we have witnessed here this evening is way beyond my wildest imagination. How you assembled a team of people and manipulated them into joining you in this shocking charade is utterly baffling."

"I'll admit that it was a little ambitious, Inspector."

"Ambitious? You've committed a serious crime, Mrs Churchill! And somehow you've persuaded your band of friends to do the same. A couple of them look rather familiar, actually." He cast a glance at Mrs Tuffield and Mr Veltom. "I recall feeling their collars once or twice in the distant past."

"Nothin' we ain't already served time for, Inspector," said Mr Veltom. "The important thing is, Mrs Churchill 'ere's found evidence of a crime."

"That's right, Mr Veltom," Churchill said proudly. "We found several items in Mr Lidcup's safe that don't belong to him. As you know, I have long suspected that Mr Spooner's secret jam recipe was stored there, and not only have I recovered it tonight, but I also found Mrs Higginbath's stolen porcelain figurine. Something she reported stolen to you about three weeks ago, I believe. May I ask what steps you took to look for it?"

"None of this excuses you for breaking and entering, Mrs Churchill!" scolded the inspector. "This is an extremely serious crime!"

"No one has been hurt by our actions."

"I beg to differ. Poor Brian Whiplark over there looks to be in a significant amount of pain after dangling from the ceiling for half the night, Miles Veltom sprained his ankle trying to rescue him and the security guard, Robert Doublet, was sat on by an eighteen-stone youth for a good ten minutes. It's not good enough, Mrs Churchill. I'm afraid I'm going to have to arrest you."

"Without arresting the man who stole the jam recipe and Mrs Higginbath's figurine? You need to take a look in his safe yourself, Inspector. I have no doubt that there are numerous other stolen items inside."

"That's a matter for the police, Mrs Churchill. Not you."

"With all due respect, Inspector Mappin, the police haven't been a great help in solving any of these crimes. How long would Mrs Higginbath's figurine have been sitting in Mr Lidcup's safe if we hadn't found it? Until he sold it again? The residents of Compton Poppleford deserve better."

"Any perceived inadequacy of the local constabulary's cannot be used to excuse vigilantism, Mrs Churchill," reprimanded Inspector Mappin. "The fact is, you masterminded a break-in and took it upon yourself to find what you perceived to be profits of crime. Whether Mr Lidcup has committed a crime or not is for a jury to decide. Not you, Mrs Churchill."

"Fine, Inspector. You may arrest me, and I'm quite sure that it will be widely reported in the local newspaper tomorrow. And what do you suppose the residents will think of Mr Lidcup then? A respectable businessman – a pillar of the community – found to have been keeping stolen goods in his safe? Everyone will be asking questions of Mr Lidcup and pointing the finger at him."

The factory owner stepped forward and adjusted his tie. "I'm sure we can find a way to solve all this without making a big song and dance about it, Mappin. Perhaps we could come to some sort of agreement."

"I'm not making a song and dance, Mr Lidcup. Let me just run through the list of misdemeanours Mrs Churchill and her companions have committed this evening. Picking the lock on the factory gate, entering the building unlawfully through a window in the roof, forcing open another window to gain unlawful access, picking the lock on your office door, Mr Lidcup, and then entering said office and breaking open a safe in that same office before removing its contents without permission."

"We only removed what we knew didn't belong to him," said Mrs Churchill. "We haven't actually stolen anything."

"Not to mention the fact that a security guard has been assaulted."

"Oliver only sat on him!" said Mrs Tuffield, having finished tending to the injured men.

"The security guard was unlawfully detained." Inspector Mappin made a note of this in his notebook. "He was impeded from going about his lawful business. I think it's safe to say, Mr Lidcup, that all of this deserves a very big song and dance indeed."

"I don't dispute what you're saying, Mappin, and I'm most upset about this evening's events myself. But there can be no doubt that Mrs Churchill has discovered certain items of interest in my safe. If word were to get out about those items, there could be a significant risk to my reputation. As a gentleman with an important role in this village, a stain on my reputation wouldn't help anyone, would it? I like to think there may be room for a little more discussion here."

"Oh, yes," said Churchill. "I'd like to have a discussion. Perhaps you can tell me, Mr Lidcup, when you learned that Jeremy Spooner had been speaking to the *Compton Poppleford Gazette* about your theft of his recipe?"

"What?"

"Did the editor, Mr Trollope, accidentally let it slip to you?"

"I have no idea what you're talking about, Mrs Churchill."

"A newspaper article on that subject would have been highly embarrassing for a gentleman with an important role in the village, wouldn't you agree?"

"I really don't see what any of this has to do with you breaking into my factory, Mrs Churchill."

"Mr Spooner was silenced!"

"Are you suggesting that I murdered him?"

"Where were you the night before his death, Mr Lidcup?"

"If I recall correctly, I was in Honiton when it all happened, because I remember hearing about it shortly after I got off the train."

"You were in Honiton?"

"Yes, in Devon. Striking up a new deal with a customer there. I'd have to check the dates in my diary, but it's just over there in my office if you'd like to take a look, Mrs Churchill. I believe your friend has kindly unlocked the door for us."

Chapter 32

"The shame, Pembers. The embarrassment!" said Churchill the following day.

"The shame and embarrassment of what?"

"Accusing Mr Lidcup of murder when he wasn't even in the county at the time! Why, oh why, didn't I think to check the date of Mr Spooner's murder in his diary while Mrs Tuffield was breaking into his safe?"

"You had a lot to think about at the time. Anyway, what if he's lying?"

"He clearly wasn't. He's already asked Inspector Mappin to confirm his account with the chap he was meeting in Honiton. And to confirm it with the hotel he stayed at, too. He wouldn't be so bold if he had something to hide." Churchill lifted her head from her desk and crammed another jam tart into her mouth.

"I think you're being too hard on yourself, Mrs Churchill."

"We were rumbled! The plan was to get in and out of that factory without being seen. We might even have managed it if the sleeping draught in the cake had lasted a little longer and Mr Whiplark had taken a longer rope."

"You found the stolen jam recipe. That was the goal of the mission, wasn't it? And as luck would have it, you found Mrs Higginbath's naughty ornament, too."

Churchill eyed the figurine sitting on her desk next to the plate of jam tarts. "That's something, I suppose. Have you told Mrs Higginbath yet?"

"Yes. I telephoned her first thing this morning and she was ever so pleased. I don't know why you're feeling so downhearted, Mrs Churchill. We're lucky Mr Lidcup was so ashamed of his actions that he refused to press charges for the break-in. And his close friendship with Mr Trollope will ensure that Smithy Miggins won't print a word of our adventures in the *Compton Poppleford Gazette*. No one else need know about us getting caught in the jam factory. As far as I'm concerned, there's no shame or embarrassment involved at all."

Heavy footsteps sounded on the staircase.

"There's only one person that can be, Pembers." Churchill grabbed another jam tart to prepare herself.

The door to the office was flung open. "There it is!"

In one swift movement, the figurine was swept up from Churchill's desk and clasped tightly to Mrs Higginbath's bosom. Churchill felt even more uneasy when she saw the librarian attempt a smile.

"I heard you found it inside the jam factory." Mrs Higginbath sat down in eager anticipation of Churchill's explanation.

"Jam factory?"

"Yes! I heard you assembled a team of people and broke in to save my figurine!"

"To save it?"

"Yes! Come now, Mrs Churchill. It's not like you to be

humble about your achievements. Oh, and before I forget…" Mrs Higginbath rested the ornament on Churchill's desk while she opened her handbag and pulled something out of it. "I'd like to present you with a reading ticket for Compton Poppleford Library, Mrs Churchill."

"Really? That's very kind of you indeed, Mrs Higginbath." She took the ticket and placed it proudly in her drawer.

"It was the least I could do after you managed to find Bonnie and Beau."

"Bonnie and Beau?"

"That's what I like to call my courting couple." She picked the figurine up once more. "I won't let them out of my sight again."

"How did you know about the jam factory?"

"Everyone knows about the jam factory."

"Oh, great." Churchill helped herself to another jam tart.

"Has Mr Lidcup been locked up?"

"No. Why do you ask?"

"He stole my figurine!"

"Yes, he did. You'll have to take it up with Inspector Mappin, I'm afraid. He's responsible for all that."

Mrs Higginbath got to her feet. "I shall indeed. I won't rest until that man is behind bars!"

"Good. Go and give Mappin a hard time over it."

"Oh, I shall!"

"It's a shame I'm too worn out to go and watch Mrs Higginbath tear a strip off Inspector Mappin," said Churchill once the librarian had left.

"She thinks you're quite the hero now, and you finally have a reading ticket for the library! Just think of all those novels you can borrow. You won't have to rely on Mrs Thonnings any longer."

"I must admit that I'd quite like to read the follow-up to *Forbidden Obsession*."

"You should do that, Mrs Churchill. It'll cheer you up."

"I'm afraid it won't, Pembers."

"Why not?"

"Because the only thing that could cheer me up now is finding out who murdered Mr Spooner. Even after all this work we've put in, we still have no idea who did it!"

Chapter 33

"THANK YOU SO VERY MUCH," said Mrs Spooner, standing on her doorstep with the stolen jam recipe in her hand. "Jeremy would be over the moon if he knew it had been returned to its rightful home. I can't tell you how grateful I am, Mrs Churchill."

"Your hunch about Mr Lidcup was right all along."

"He'll be locked up for Jeremy's murder now, won't he?"

"No."

"Why ever not?"

"For the simple reason that he didn't do it, Mrs Spooner."

"Oh! Who did then?"

"That's the million-dollar question."

"Dollars?"

"I realise we use pound sterling in this country. It's just an expression."

"I wish I could earn a million dollars by answering it."

"So do I, Mrs Spooner. Actually, I don't even want the

million dollars; I just want to find out who murdered your husband."

"I wouldn't turn down a million dollars quite so swiftly," said Pemberley. "I'd be extremely happy to receive such a large sum of money."

"So would I," agreed Mrs Spooner. "Wouldn't it be wonderful? I'd enjoy a lovely holiday by the sea."

"I'm beginning to wish I hadn't introduced the expression to our conversation," said Churchill. "The fact of the matter remains that we must find the person who callously loosened the bolts on the tenor bell and caused it to fall on your husband's head, Mrs Spooner. You mentioned that he was having an extramarital affair. I assume you never confronted him about it."

"Oh, no! I didn't know how to. Besides, I never did like confrontations. I hoped it would all blow over and be forgotten about soon enough."

"You never discussed it at all with your husband?"

"No. We were happily married for twenty-seven years and I didn't want to ruin what we had."

"But you must have felt upset about it."

She pushed out her lower lip. "A little."

"Angry?"

"Sometimes."

"Vengeful?"

She nodded. "Yes, I did feel vengeful now and again. Oh, how I hate to admit that I ever harboured such feelings now that he's gone! He's not even here to defend himself."

"You're perfectly entitled to feel the way you feel, Mrs Spooner. If you felt vengeful—"

"I refused to darn his socks for a whole week once."

"Is that so?"

"I was so upset about it, you see. I never explained why

I wasn't darning his socks; I just came up with an excuse not to. Said I was busy or something along those lines."

"That was your act of revenge?"

"That and a few other silly things. Only ever small, silly things, Mrs Churchill, but I feel so guilty about them now."

"What about bigger vengeful things?"

The widow took a step back and gave Churchill a cautious glance. "No," she said firmly. "Refusing to darn his socks was about as vengeful as I ever got."

"Good morning, ladies!" said Mrs Thonnings with a smile as they entered her shop. "I suppose I should still be in a sulk after you suggested I'd had an affair with Jeremy Spooner, Mrs Churchill, but I want to hear all about your exploits at the jam factory!"

"What exploits?"

"Don't be coy, Mrs Churchill. It doesn't suit you."

"How did you hear about these supposed exploits?"

"They're the talk of the whole village!"

"It's a shame nobody has anything else to talk about."

"But it's so exciting! I've heard all about how you got in through the roof, Mrs Churchill. You sailed in on a rope and snatched Mrs Higginbath's priceless ornament from the evil clutches of Mr Lidcup!"

"Pure fiction, Mrs Thonnings."

"Even if it is, why not enjoy the moment, Mrs Churchill? You won't often hear people singing your praises quite so loudly."

"There's certainly some truth in that. Now, Mrs Thonnings, I've been feeling the need to stitch a sampler. An alphabet sampler just like the ones I used to sew as a child. I need thinking time, you see, and I recall that stitching a sampler helps one's brain to tick over."

"I can't disagree with that, Mrs Churchill. Would you like to come and pick out some embroidery threads?"

"Just fill a bag with them, Mrs Thonnings. Pick any colours you like."

"What fun!"

"Precisely. I need to shut myself away with a needle and thread, and muse."

"A needle, some thread and a muse?"

"Just *muse*. As in, 'to muse'."

"It's a verb, Mrs Thonnings," said Pemberley. "It means 'to think deeply about something'."

"Lovely. I'll put some threads in a bag for you."

"Can I join you when you shut yourself away with your needle and thread and your muse, Mrs Churchill? I need to finish my prayer cushion."

The two ladies were walking along the high street back to their office.

"What an excellent idea, Pembers. We'll put a sign up on the door saying 'Closed' so no one can disturb us while we stitch."

Chapter 34

After a quiet day of stitching, musing and eating cake, Churchill felt she had come up with a reasonably robust theory about the murder of Mr Spooner.

"All I can do now is put it to the villagers tomorrow," she said to Pemberley, scanning her notes. "Then we'll find out where it gets us."

"I must say that you spent far more time using your pen than your needle," commented Pemberley. "You've only finished one letter of your alphabet sampler."

"I made a start on the B, but I had to unpick it again. I may not have completed it, Pembers, but the important thing is, it got me thinking. That's all I needed; just something to get me thinking."

"I've finished my prayer cushion."

"Have you? Let's see it, then!"

"It's come out a bit smaller than I'd planned, but at least I'll have enough thread left over to make another one. Another five or six, even."

"Gosh, Pembers, it is small. Even a child would struggle to kneel on that!"

"Oh dear, do you think so? I got a bit impatient and just wanted to get it finished, you see."

"I know the feeling."

"The vicar will be so disappointed in me."

"Just don't give it to him."

"But I have to! I told him I'd make one."

"You did, but he didn't seem particularly bothered about it. Give it to someone who has a greater need of it."

"Such as?"

"I think it's a perfect-sized pillow."

"For a gnome?"

"No. For a dog."

"Oh, yes!" Pemberley's face instantly brightened. "Oswald can have it in his bed!"

"Absolutely."

"And it's perfect because I embroidered a picture of him on it!"

"That's Oswald?"

"Yes."

"You're holding it upside down."

"Am I? No, I'm not. That's definitely the right way up."

"Oh, excellent. I'm sure he'll love it."

"He will indeed!"

"Right, then. Where shall we hold our little gathering?"

"At the jam factory?"

"Goodness, no. I've had enough of that place for the time being. How about the churchyard?"

"We've had a similar little gathering there before."

"There's no harm in doing so again. It is, after all, where our story begins. Just before you start arranging it, though, I need to take a little walk."

"What for?"

"To work out a few important timings. If I'm lucky, I might find another witness or two as well."

Chapter 35

A SMALL CROWD was beginning to gather in the sunny churchyard the following morning.

"What's going on?" asked the sexton, a gaunt man dressed in black.

"Mrs Churchill's about to make one of her announcements," said Mrs Thonnings cheerily. "I love it when she does this."

"Just watch where you're standing," he barked. "I don't want any of the graves getting trampled."

Churchill and Pemberley watched as a steady stream of people filed in through the church gate and up the path. Oswald sniffed each new arrival and happily accepted several pats on the head.

Mr Whiplark sauntered in with Mr Barnfather, while Mrs Lillywhite was accompanied by Oliver, and Mr Veltom arrived arm in arm with Mrs Tuffield.

"It looks like some sort of romance has blossomed," Churchill whispered to Pemberley.

"Perhaps the jam factory heist was the catalyst!"

"Perhaps it was."

The upper window of a nearby cottage opened and Mr Purseglove's beady-eyed face peered out. When Churchill gave him a little wave, he slammed the window shut again.

Mrs Higginbath and Mrs Mullard arrived next, shortly followed by a quartet of bell-ringers: Mr Thurkell, Mr Cogg, Mr Linney and Mr Melding. Smithy Miggins lingered at the edge of the crowd, his notepad ready. Mrs Spooner was accompanied by the vicar, and just as Churchill was ready to begin, Mr and Mrs Purseglove scampered up the path.

"Ready whenever you are, Mrs Churchill," said Inspector Mappin. "I'll stand quite close to Mr Whiplark so I can clap the handcuffs on him before he has a chance to get away."

"Why are you so sure it was him?"

"Who else could it have been?"

"Why haven't you already arrested him if he's your chief suspect?"

"I just need a little more evidence, Mrs Churchill which I presume you're about to provide."

She arranged her papers and her heart gave a little skip as she noticed the glowering face of Mr Lidcup among those assembled. She knew he would never forgive her for breaking into his factory. The best she could do was deliver her theory and then get away for a while. Perhaps a short holiday in Weymouth would fit the bill.

She cleared her throat. "Is everybody ready?"

There was a general murmur of assent.

"Good, then I'll begin. As you're aware, the local belfry man, Mr Jeremy Spooner, sadly lost his life in this church when the tenor bell came loose from its fittings and fell on top of him. It didn't take the local constabulary long to notice that the bolts holding the bell in place had been tampered with."

Inspector Mappin gave a proud nod.

"What had initially appeared to be an accident was, in fact, murder." She paused for dramatic effect, then continued. "At the time of his death, Jeremy Spooner was not a popular man. His fellow bell-ringers had resigned their positions and taken up with the bell-ringing team in nearby South Bungerly."

"Why'd they do that?" a male voice called out.

"My hands couldn't take it anymore!" elderly Mr Cogg replied. "He had us ringing quarter peals every evening!"

"That's twelve hundred and fifty changes," clarified Mr Barnfather.

"And if I ever hear 'Double Norwich Court Bob Major' again, I'll lose my mind," Mr Linney piped up.

"Just some of the reasons, straight from the mouths of the bell-ringers themselves," said Churchill. "I hope that answers your question, sir."

"Seven o'clock on a Sunday morning!" shouted Mr Purseglove. "Can't a chap get a bit of peace first thing on the Sabbath?"

"Well, you certainly have a bit of peace now," said Mrs Churchill. "I'll discuss you in a minute, Mr Purseglove—"

"Discuss me? Whatever for?"

"I'll explain in a moment. For the time being, I'm busy discussing the bell-ringers. Now, where was I? Ah yes, all the bell-ringers had left for South Bungerly. Seven disgruntled bell-ringers; likely candidates for meting out some sort of revenge, wouldn't you say?"

"No!" boomed Mr Barnfather.

"It's like I told you, Mrs Churchill," Mr Cogg called out. "None of us would ever have damaged one of our beloved bells."

"Yes, I realise they were your beloved bells, Mr Cogg.

You didn't care much for Mr Spooner, but the bells were a different matter."

"Exactly!"

"So if we're to assume that the bell-ringers would never have harmed their own bells, that leads us on to the other villagers who bore some sort of resentment toward Mr Spooner. Forgive me if I'm phrasing this incorrectly, Mr Purseglove, but didn't you once threaten to wrap a bell rope around Mr Spooner's neck?"

"Yes, I did. And I'm proud of it!"

Gasps resounded through the crowd and Mrs Spooner gave a pained cry.

"I know what you're all thinking," he said to the crowd, "but I was a desperate man. I was so sick of those bells! Ringing and ringing and ringing—"

"Quite astonishing what a man can be driven to in situations like this, wouldn't you say, Mr Purseglove?"

"Oh, yes. I can quite understand how someone might end up murdering someone else."

"I see."

"It could be very tempting indeed!"

"Thank you, Mr Purseglove."

"I didn't do it, though."

"You live very close to the church, don't you?"

"Right by it, yes. That's my house just there." He pointed at it.

"So close by, in fact, that you could have snuck out in the dead of night, climbed the bell tower and loosened the bolts on the tenor bell in no time at all."

"I could've done, but I didn't."

"But you were well placed to, and you had a motive."

"Are you suggesting that I killed him, Mrs Churchill?"

"Did you?"

"Of course not!"

"Very well. Let's not forget that for the murderer to have committed this crime, he or she required some prior knowledge of the way the bells were attached to the bell frame in the belfry."

All eyes turned toward Mr Whiplark.

"Oh, 'ere we go again!" he lamented. "The finger points at me just 'cause I were the steeple keeper. I'll admit that I knows better than anyone 'ow them bells work. But does that mean I went 'n' fiddled about with them bolts? No, it don't." He folded his arms. "After all I've done for you, Miss Churchley – 'angin' from the ceilin' and all the rest of it – here I am, still bein' accused o' murder!"

"You had a motive, Mr Whiplark. You were one of those disgruntled bell-ringers."

"Yeah, I was. But didn't you say just now, Miss Churchley, 'ow we never would've done nothin' to 'arm them bells? I'll tell you it again, too. They're me pride and joy! I've given you an alibi 'n' all."

"Your horse."

A snigger of laughter spread through the crowd.

"Better'n no alibi!" retorted Mr Whiplark angrily.

"I thought Mr Lidcup was the murderer?" someone called out.

"So did I," replied Churchill. "For a little while, at least."

"He stole my husband's secret jam recipe!" blurted Mrs Spooner. "Poor Jeremy died not knowing what had happened to it!"

"And my figurine!" called Mrs Higginbath.

"D'yer mean the naughty ornament?" someone asked.

More laughter rippled through the crowd.

"I'd like to know why it's being called that!" she retorted.

"At least you didn't die without knowing what had happened to it!" cried Mrs Spooner.

"I'd like to make a call to order," said Churchill. "I've almost finished now."

"Who done it?" came a voice.

"I have a theory to share with you once everyone has calmed down."

"We've calmed down now," said Mrs Thonnings.

"Good. Now, there's a rather sensitive matter I must broach, and that is the issue of Mr Spooner's infidelity."

"Mr Spooner had a bit on the side?" said Mr Purseglove in disbelief. "Well I never!"

"Will you please stop interrupting?" chided Churchill. "His brave and courageous widow discovered that he had been committing adultery but told me she knew very little about his mistress. Nothing at all, in fact. As you can imagine, it's been rather difficult for us to identify this mystery woman. However, I can now reveal that the lady in question is Mrs Tuffield."

The announcement was met with surprised gasps.

The watch repairer's face turned a deep red.

"It was an item Mrs Spooner found in her husband's shed that gave me an important clue," continued Churchill. "The poor widow described how she had found a lady's handbag hidden behind his workbench. Within the handbag, among various small personal items, was a stethoscope. Mrs Spooner made the quite valid assumption that the owner of the handbag might work as a doctor's secretary, but while investigating this possibility, my trusty assistant and I could find no suitable candidate.

"You all know Mrs Tuffield as the village watch repairer, but she is also extremely adept at cracking safes. You may not know this, but an important part of a safe breaker's kit is a stethoscope, which is used to listen to the subtle vibrations and turns of the safe mechanism."

Mrs Tuffield laughed. "A handbag is found with a stethoscope inside and you immediately assume it was mine?"

"Do you deny it?"

The watch repairer contorted her face one way and then another. "No," she eventually said.

"Thank you, Mrs Tuffield. Your admission brings me neatly on to the next part of my theory."

"Is Mrs Tuffield the murderer?" asked Mr Purseglove.

"Please allow me to finish, Mr Purseglove. It's important to note that Mrs Tuffield has a great fear of heights. This was something I heard her say several times during a recent outing we undertook together."

"When you broke into the jam factory?" someone asked.

"I can neither confirm nor deny it. Anyway, I decided that if Mrs Tuffield hated heights, she probably wouldn't have chosen to climb up the bell tower. The murderer had to be someone who didn't mind heights. Someone like Mr Whiplark, for example."

"It wasn't me!"

"And certainly someone with a knowledge of the bells and the way they work," continued Churchill. "So I shall put it to you all now that it was Mr Veltom who murdered Mr Spooner."

"What?!" Mr Veltom exclaimed.

Everyone turned to look at the curly-haired, thick-whiskered man.

He began to chuckle. "I don't think I've ever 'eard anythin' so funny in all me days."

Mrs Tuffield removed her arm from his and gently edged away.

"What evidence yer got?" he asked sharply.

"You're going to have to explain yourself, Mrs Churchill," said Inspector Mappin. "Mr Veltom may be a lock picker and a convicted criminal, but I very much doubt he's a murderer."

"Well, the motive is quite obvious," replied Churchill. "Mr Veltom is in love with Mrs Tuffield. That soon became evident while we were carrying out our recent visit to the jam factory. Mr Spooner was a rival for Mrs Tuffield's affections, and Mr Veltom hoped Mrs Tuffield would welcome him with open arms once he had rid himself of his rival."

"I almost did!" she retorted, staring at Mr Veltom with a look of horror.

"There ain't no evidence!" he hollered.

"My advice, Inspector, would be to apprehend him," said Churchill. "Although he denies carrying out the murder, I'm fairly confident that he'll try to run away in just a moment. Oh dear, it appears he already has."

Mr Veltom had made a dash for the churchyard path and was heading swiftly toward the kissing gate.

Inspector Mappin charged after him, but the bell-ringer was faster.

"Catch him, someone!" cried out Churchill.

Oliver Lillywhite performed a rugby tackle on the absconding Mr Veltom, wrapping his large arms around the bell-ringer's knees and felling him like a tree. Inspector Mappin tumbled over the two men, losing his hat in the process. After a brief scuffle, he managed to fasten his handcuffs around Mr Veltom's wrists.

The inspector got to his feet and hauled Mr Veltom up with the assistance of Mr Barnfather.

"Just before I arrest him, Mrs Churchill," he called out,

"have you any concrete evidence that this man carried out the crime?"

"A flickering light was seen in St Swithun's bell tower at three o'clock on the morning of Mr Spooner's murder," replied Churchill. "You witnessed the light, did you not, Mrs Harris?"

The buck-toothed lady gave an enthusiastic nod.

"There's no doubt that the murderer would have required a light to find his way up the winding staircase and vandalise the bell in the belfry. Having learned that Mr Veltom lived next door to the Pig and Scythe public house, I traced the route he would have taken that fateful morning. It's a walk of about fifteen minutes. Now, I realise few people would have been around at that hour, which is probably why Mr Veltom chose it to carry out his act of sabotage. However, I did speak to the fishmonger who unlocks the doors to his yard very early each morning to receive his delivery. He told me he had seen Mr Veltom walking in the direction of the church. This isn't concrete evidence that Mr Veltom went on to climb the bell tower and loosen the bolts on the bell, but I'm sure you'll agree, Inspector, that it does put him in an interesting location at an interesting time."

"That's good enough for now, Mrs Churchill. Come along, Mr Veltom. You've some questions to answer down at the station."

Chapter 36

"Thank you, Miss Churchley!" called Mr Whiplark. "Now everyone knows it weren't me!"

"Or me!" announced a smug-looking Mr Lidcup. "And to celebrate the apprehension of the murderer, I'd like to offer every single villager a complimentary jar of plum jam! Limited to one per household, of course. Merely present yourself at my factory between eight and five o'clock tomorrow, and a free jar shall be yours!"

His offer received a muted response from the crowd, the various members of which were already shuffling away.

"Well done, Mrs Churchill and Miss Pemberley," said Mrs Thonnings, approaching the two ladies with a smile on her face. "And Oswald, of course." She gave the little dog a pat. "I don't know how you do it!"

"Neither do I," replied Churchill, resting her back against Sir Ronald Eversley's tomb. "I'm exhausted."

"I still can't believe that a bell-ringer could have caused such damage to the church bells," said the vicar, sadly shaking his head. "What is this world coming to?"

"At least Jeremy can rest in peace now," said Mrs

Spooner. "I'm just struggling to understand how Mr Veltom could have done such a thing."

"Likewise, Mrs Spooner," he said. "Until recently, I had complete trust in him."

"There's no justice in this world," grumbled Mrs Higginbath as she sauntered up to the ladies. "Mr Veltom will be locked up, yet the one who stole my figurine is to walk about as a free man!"

"Surely he'll receive some sort of punishment?" said Mrs Thonnings.

"Inspector Mappin tells me he's to appear in front of the magistrates later this week, but he'll probably be given a fine rather than a lengthy jail term. Law and order has gone soft these days."

"The important thing is that a dangerous murderer will be locked up," said the vicar. "If you ask me, he should also pay for the repairs to my church. The chances of that are fairly slim, though. I'll have to ask the bishop for the money."

"Haven't you asked him yet?" queried Churchill.

"No. It's taken me a good few weeks to pluck up the courage."

"I hope it all gets repaired quickly so we can hear the pleasant sound of church bells ringing again soon," said Pemberley.

"There may be a few people who disagree with you on that front, Miss Pemberley," said Churchill.

"As long as they're rung in moderation, I'm sure all will be fine," said the vicar.

Mrs Higginbath withdrew a small notebook from her pocket. "While you're all here, I might as well take the opportunity to remind you of the library books that are currently due for renewal. Mrs Thonnings, *Careless Desire* needs to be returned by Friday."

The haberdasher nodded.

"*The Havana Heist* needs to be returned tomorrow, Miss Pemberley."

"Can I renew it? I haven't found the time to finish it yet."

"That all depends on whether anyone else has reserved it. I'll have to check when I return to the library. You've two books out on loan, Vicar. The first is *Ancient Christian Commentary on Scripture.*"

The vicar nodded.

"And the second is *A Guide to Large Firearms.*"

"Goodness, Vicar! I wasn't aware that you had such an interest in guns," said Churchill.

"I don't," he stammered. "I think there must be a mistake."

"No mistake." Mrs Higginbath consulted her notebook once again. "It was borrowed two weeks and three days ago on your ticket."

"Oh, that was for my nephew."

"On *your* ticket? Your nephew should be using his own ticket!"

Churchill gave Pemberley a gentle nudge to suggest that this would be a good time to slip away.

"Do you feel as exhausted as I do by all this, Pembers?" Churchill asked as they walked back along the high street to their office. Oswald was happily trotting alongside them wearing a large daisy Pemberley had tucked into his collar.

"Yes, I feel very tired."

"I sometimes wonder if we're getting a little too old for all this."

"That's impossible! There's plenty of life in us yet."

"I hope you're right, my trusty assistant."

"Maybe you just need a holiday, Mrs Churchill."

"That's exactly what I need. It's what we both need, in fact. And Oswald, of course."

"A few days in Weymouth, perhaps?"

"It's as if you can read my mind, Pembers. I was thinking the very same thing yesterday. It's not easy to get to, though. It's a long train journey, and you have to change at Dorchester."

"I know a lady who makes regular deliveries there. Perhaps she could give us a lift."

"Please tell me you're joking, Pembers. I'd rather find myself dangling from the roof of Mr Lidcup's jam factory than get inside that van again!"

The End

Thank You

Thank you for reading *Fiasco at the Jam Factory*, I really hope you enjoyed it!

Would you like to know when I release new books? Here are some ways to stay updated:

- Join my mailing list and receive the short story *A Troublesome Case*: emilyorgan.com/a-troublesome-case
- Like my Facebook page: facebook.com/emilyorganwriter
- Follow me on Goodreads: goodreads.com/emily_organ
- Follow me on BookBub: bookbub.com/authors/emily-organ
- View my other books here: emilyorgan.com

And if you have a moment, I would be very grateful if you would leave a quick review of *Fiasco at the Jam Factory* online. Honest reviews of my books help other readers discover them too!

Get a free short mystery

~

Want more of Churchill & Pemberley? Get a copy of my free short mystery *A Troublesome Case* and sit down to enjoy a thirty minute read.

Churchill and Pemberley are on the train home from a shopping trip when they're caught up with a theft from a suitcase. Inspector Mappin accuses them of stealing the valuables, but in an unusual twist of fate the elderly sleuths are forced to come to his aid!

Visit my website to claim your FREE copy:

emilyorgan.com/a-troublesome-case

Or scan this code:

Get a free short mystery

The Penny Green Series

~

Also by Emily Organ. A series of mysteries set in Victorian London featuring the intrepid Fleet Street reporter, Penny Green.

What readers are saying:

"A Victorian Delight!"

"Good clean mystery in an enjoyable historical setting"

"If you are unfamiliar with the Penny Green Series, acquaint yourselves immediately!"

Books in the Penny Green Series:

Limelight

The Rookery

The Maid's Secret

The Inventor

Curse of the Poppy

The Bermondsey Poisoner

The Penny Green Series

An Unwelcome Guest
Death at the Workhouse
The Gang of St Bride's
Murder in Ratcliffe
The Egyptian Mystery

The Augusta Peel Series

~

Meet Augusta Peel, an amateur sleuth with a mysterious past.

She's a middle-aged book repairer who chaperones young ladies and minds other people's pets in her spare time. But there's more to Augusta than meets the eye.

Detective Inspector Fisher of Scotland Yard was well acquainted with Augusta during the war. In 1920s London, no one wishes to discuss those times but he decides Augusta can be relied upon when a tricky murder case comes his way.

Death in Soho is a 1920s cozy mystery set in London in 1921. Featuring actual and fictional locations, the story takes place in colourful Soho and bookish Bloomsbury. A read for fans of page-turning, light mysteries with historical detail!

Find out more here: emilyorgan.com/augusta-peel

Printed in Great Britain
by Amazon

75017960R00142